Fighting *with* Whales

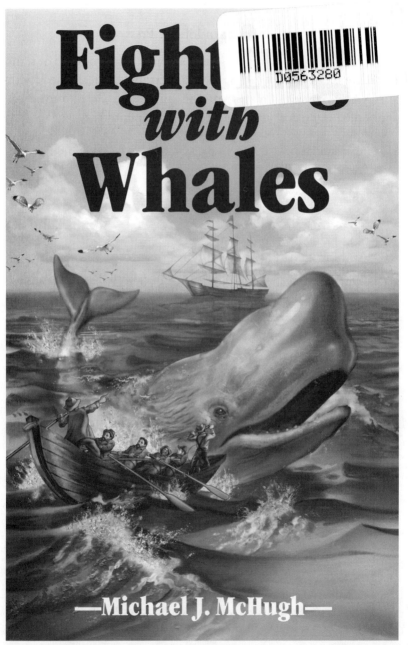

—Michael J. McHugh—

CHRISTIAN LIBERTY PRESS

ARLINGTON HEIGHTS, ILLINOIS

A publication of
Christian Liberty Press
502 West Euclid Avenue
Arlington Heights, Illinois 60004

Author: Michael J. McHugh
Editors: Edward J. Shewan, Diane Olson
Design: Bob Fine
Cover art: Chris Ellithorpe

Ad maiorem

Dei gloriam

CHRISTIAN LIBERTY PRESS
502 West Euclid Avenue
Arlington Heights, Illinois 60004
www.christianlibertypress.com
ISBN 1-930367-85-6

Song Credits: The song that appears in chapter nine entitled, *Carlingford*, is copyrighted by Tommy Makem.

Image Credits: Grateful acknowledgement is given to Dover Publications for use of their copyrighted images which appear on pages 24, 30, 34, 36, 39, 42, 45, 48, 52, 53, 54, 63, 80, 84, 99, and 100.

Printed in the United States of America

—*Dedication*—

This book is dedicated to the memory of my dear departed pastor and friend, Dr. Paul D. Lindstrom, (1939-2002). In the gracious providence of God, I was saved under the preaching of Pastor Lindstrom in the 1970s, and in the 1980s I was encouraged by this faithful minister to begin my first writing project.

All glory to the triune God of Scripture for granting me the privilege to labor alongside one of the truly great educational reformers of the twentieth century—Dr. Paul D. Lindstrom.

Contents

—Introduction—

I t took a great deal of determination and courage to set out on a whaling voyage in the nineteenth century. Most ship owners required crew members to sign on for at least a two-year voyage and sometimes demanded as long as a four-year commitment.

The anxiety that many men felt as a result of being taken away from their families or friends for extended periods was also punctuated by significant periods of utter boredom when the seas were quiet and the whales were scarce. If the difficulties associated with leaving loved ones and dealing with boredom did not crush you emotionally, then the routine demands of being part of a crew of whaling men was often enough to break you physically. A ceaseless array of tedious watches and hard labor amidst the scorching sun or stormy gale was the common lot of whaling men. Perhaps the greatest threat to life and limb, however, came during the actual act of hunting or processing the whales themselves. Unless, of course, you factor in the food that sailors were expected to eat, which was often a threat to their health due to its spoiled or rancid condition.

All in all, it should not be surprising to discover that most sailors only shipped out on one long whaling voyage during their career. A few hearty men, however, managed to find a way to love this strenuous life and stayed at sea over the long haul. Some of these men began their whaling careers as cabin boys and, eventually, worked their way up to the point where they became captains.

The story you are about to read is a fascinating account of two young men, from very different backgrounds, who experience the adventure of whaling during the mid-nineteenth century. It is a story not only of high sea adventure and hardship, but also of friendship, love, and God's redeeming grace.

Prior to the Civil War in the United States, most Americans living on the eastern seaboard, particularly in New England, considered whaling a very important business enterprise. During these bygone days, the American people relied greatly upon the whaling industry to supply them with useful products such as whale oil and whalebone. Towns such as New Bedford, Mystic, and Nantucket became prosperous as a result of the popularity of whale products.

In modern American society, few people understand why men risked their lives and endured long periods of loneliness simply to hunt for whales. It is the hope of the author that readers of this book will be able to appreciate the daring exploits of whale men and to rightly esteem their accomplishments. May your respect for whales and whaling men grow as you consider what it was like to come face to face with a monstrous creature armed only with an iron spear and Yankee courage.

Michael J. McHugh
Arlington Heights, Illinois
2002

CHAPTER 1
Memories of My Youth

A dense fog rose slowly from the cobblestones of old New Bedford town. It was early in the spring of 1902, and my bones still ached from the dampness and cold.

As I walked slowly on, I began to view the wharf and smell the lingering aroma of rotting canvas and wood. Ninety paces ahead, I could see the tall skeletons of old ships, looking like something out of an elephant graveyard.

Many things had changed in the tiny New England town of New Bedford since the collapse of the whaling industry, but, as an old man, I could still comfort myself in the knowledge that the innkeeper still knew my name. After a long walk, I finally approached the familiar door which led into the Whaler's Inn. Moments later, much to my delight, a plump and seasoned innkeeper bellowed out my name.

"For the love of big whales, if it isn't old Jim Surrey!" spouted the proprietor of the dimly lit establishment. "What brings you in from the cold, my friend, have you a taste for a bowl of chowder this fine day?"

"No, No," I responded. "Staying away from your chowder has caused me to live into old age. My hope is to meet with my old shipmate, Timothy Dronner, and to rekindle our friendship."

"Well, if you can't have a warm stomach this day, may ye have a heartwarming gam with your friend," replied the good-natured innkeeper.

As I moved deeper into the confines of the inn, a corner booth graced with an oil lamp came before me. Sitting down, I quickly set aside my cap and cane and ordered up a hot drink. Before long, I found myself signaling to the innkeeper for another drink to be brought as I recognized the voice of an old friend coming closer to my ears.

"Hallo, Master Jim!" asserted the bright-eyed visitor named Timothy Dronner. "I hardly thought to see ye out this day considering the cold and damp."

"My old bones never could tell me what to do with my time, mate. We seldom find the time for a gam, dear friend, so I am here even though me bones are talking kinda loud these days. Sit down, then, sit down before ye fall down."

"Jim, can it truly be that we shipped out on our first voyage almost sixty years ago?" asked Timothy as he began to puff on his long-necked pipe.

"Pretty nearly so, my friend, we were but mere lads and as green as a cucumber," I responded. "Even after all these years since we have hung up our oilskins, I still can't get used to seeing New Bedford town so still and quiet. Time was when every part of town was bursting with activity."

"I know what you mean," said Timothy quickly. "I can still see Captain Flynn strolling down the wharf, top hat and all."

"It's hard to keep from thinking about the days of our youth, old friend," I added, as I began to stare into a nearby fireplace. "It all seems like a wild dream, and, at the rate our memories are fading, even the dream may soon be gone."

"We must not let the story of whaling men be capsized and lost, shipmate," said the concerned old sailor named Timothy as he turned to the crowd gathered at the inn.

Moments later, this grey-haired salt of the sea boldly stood up and addressed the curious onlookers. "Dear people of New Bedford, my name is Timothy Dronner, and I ask thee to gather 'round and lend an ear to my friend and former shipmate, Jim Surrey. He has a tale worth telling about the great days of sail and of the men who fought big whales. Fill your glasses then, and listen to my friend spin a story worth passing on to your children and grandchildren."

Slowly, people began to position themselves close to the heavy wooden table where I sat, in utter silence, still taken aback by the boldness of my friend's speech. A short time later, a small group of townspeople sat staring at me as I reluctantly resigned myself to the task of telling the story of my adventures as a whaling man.

A strange hush fell over the Whaler's Inn as I slowly proceeded to explain how I was first led to become a whaler. Amidst the clanking of glasses and shuffling of chairs, I started to take on the role of an old storyteller by lifting up my gravely voice and beginning a voyage of words.

Chapter 2
A Friendship Begun

About sixty years ago, I lived with my mother in the nearby town of Fairhaven. Many is the time that I would look across the Acushnet River toward New Bedford and watch the world's greatest whaling port receive another heavily laden vessel. Even now, if I close my eyes, I can smell the sweet odor flowing from the hundreds of barrels of whale oil that used to routinely sit on the waterfront docks of New Bedford.

As a young lad, I would listen as my mother would tell of the day that my own dear father shipped out on a three-year voyage to the Azores in search of seals and whale. Like many men before him, my father never returned alive. The word that my mother received from the ship's captain was that he took sick on the voyage out and died. Being nowhere close to land, they were forced to bury him at sea.

Many were the tears that flowed down my mother's cheeks as she labored in her spirit to accept the Almighty's will. The passing of the head of our home also meant the passing of any meaningful source of money for the household. The first winter after my father's death, we received some money from my late father's share of his last voyage. This payment of the so-called "part" of the voyage lasted but a few months, and then we hit the hard times.

My mother had to work for food and clothes for us both after the money was gone. Often her toilsome labor was rewarded by only a handful of wool, a pail of milk or some fish. Funny though, I don't recall her ever complaining about her lot.

As I grew older, both my mother and I began to work for the wealthy class of merchants and ship owners that inhabited the waterfront mansions. Life was often hard without Father, but we managed to make a living.

In my youth, it seemed as though everyone worked in the business of whaling in some manner. The shops in town serviced the needs of crews and ships alike. The coopers' shops were hard pressed to keep up with the demand for suitable barrels, and the carpenters and riggers seldom lacked employment.

Every boy in town, however, dreamed of being the captain of an ivory-trimmed bark, or at least an officer of some kind. Whenever time permitted, my friends and I would gather around the blacksmith's shop and listen to whalers tell of their adventures on the high seas. My friends and I would often argue about which whale was the biggest or most fierce as we quickly learned the names of all of the famous whales.

One spring day, in the year of our Lord 1846, as I was running an errand for my mother, I heard a loud noise coming from the direction of the blacksmith's shop. Running on, I saw two young boys fighting with each other. The one lad held a knife in his hand and the other a wooden stick.

Almost without thinking, I proceeded to pick up a large apple from a nearby fruit stand and hurl it at the boy who held the knife. My aim was unusually good that day, and I was able to hit the knife-wielding lad square in the head. Moments later, the young man lay dazed on the street in front of the blacksmith's shop.

A stout man with big arms and a short temper walked over to where the lad was lying and picked up his knife. This gentleman was the best known blacksmith in town, and he rarely spoke without good reason. You had better believe, then, that everyone who was in earshot listened carefully as he spoke.

"I won't tolerate any more trouble around my place!" shouted the disturbed shopkeeper. "If ye need to fuss and quarrel, lads, go settle your disputes in front of someone else's establishment."

Although the boy with the wooden stick seemed content

enough with the declaration of the blacksmith, the lad on the ground appeared to receive the news with considerably less glee, for the shopkeeper proceeded to toss a bucket of ice cold water upon him.

The crowd on the street, including myself, thought the whole scene was quite amusing. After I regained my composure, I walked over to the lad who, moments before, had been staring down the length of a knife blade.

"Many thanks, stranger," said the grateful boy. "My name is Timothy Dronner, but my friends call me Tim. What be your name?"

"The name is Jim Surrey. What brings you into town this day, besides fighting? You strike me as a greenhorn from the country!"

"Where I come from is none of your business, and as for fighting, well, let's just say that I've had enough fighting for one day. I came to find work as a whaler. I have always dreamed of catching big fish," responded the lad, confidently.

"Well enough, stranger. But how do ye hope to become a whale man when you do not as yet know that whales are mammals, not fish? Besides, you are not yet eighteen, as near as I can tell."

"I'll sort that out in good time, Jim. To tell you the truth, I'm more concerned about where my next meal will come from. Do you have any more large apples that I could utilize for eating rather than throwing?"

"I'm afraid not," I chuckled. "Perhaps you would like to follow me home to see what's left in my mother's cupboard?"

"If you're inviting me to your home, then I ain't too proud to follow," said the thankful stranger.

As the crowd finally dispersed, the two of us walked quickly toward my mother's humble dwelling on the other side of the bay. After several minutes, I asked my new found friend how he was planning to eat without money or employment.

"Oh, I guess I underestimated the difficulties," Tim responded. "I had lately determined that I would set to begging for my food.

But I must confess that a sick feeling came over me when I thought of begging."

The young stranger went on to explain how he had offered his services to several townspeople in a wild sort of way with no success. His shame was lessened to some degree only because he knew that he was willing to work, if only someone would give him the opportunity.

As my new companion and I traveled on, we stopped at a local dry goods shop to pick up a few things for my dear old mother. Here I purchased a pound of tea, flour, sugar, and butter. I also procured a few hard biscuits and some honey as snacks for the remaining trip home.

In the space of an hour after we left the dry goods shop, young Tim and I reached my mother's home. She was sitting at the kitchen table when we went in, with a large Bible before her and a pair of horn spectacles on her nose. I could see that she had been out gathering wood during my absence, for a strong fire burned in the grate and the tea kettle was singing merrily thereon.

"I've brought a friend to see you, Mother," said I.

"Good-day, mistress," said the unemployed lad awkwardly, sitting down on a stool near the fire. "You seem ready to have your tea."

"I expect to have it soon," replied my mother. "I hope you can stay for a cup."

"Indeed!" said the visitor, with a surprised look. "Have you anything in the kettle?"

"Nothing but water, my young friend," replied my mother.

"Why, then, mistress," continued the curious stranger, "how can you expect to have your tea so soon?"

My mother took off her spectacles, looked calmly in the young man's face, laid her hand on the Bible, and said, "Because I have been a widow woman these three years, and never once in all that time have I gone a single day without a meal. When the usual hour came, I put on my kettle to boil, for this Word tells me that 'the Lord will provide.' I expect my tea tonight because I know that my faithful son has done his best to take care of me, and that God will do the rest."

The visitor's face expressed astonishment at these words, and he continued to regard my mother with a look of wonder as I proceeded to pull out the supplies of food from my knapsack and place them on the table.

In a short time, we were all enjoying a cup of tea, and talking about the plans of my new friend to sign on a whaling ship bound for the South Seas.

"I long for adventure and a chance to make a living on the sea," insisted the self-assured visitor.

"Dying is a hard way to make a living," responded my mother in a firm yet quiet manner. "Many is the man who looked for the sea to bring him his fortune, only to find incredible hardships and a watery grave. My own husband lies at the bottom of the ocean even now."

"I regret your husband's fate, dear woman," asserted the young man soberly. "Yet I hasten to say that in hard times like these, there are few options open to a young man such as myself, seeing that my learning is no good. It's either the mines or the mill back home as I was never cut out to be a farmer like my father."

"And just how do you plan on getting hired onto a whaling vessel with no experience and nobody to sponsor your application?" questioned my mother.

"As I have already told your generous son, my dear lady, I will sort this out in good time. If you will but pray for me, madam, I am sure that something good will come my way in the Lord's good time."

"Very well, then," concluded my mother. "We will offer you our prayers and our food this fine evening. Will you be staying the night then, laddie?"

"If you are willing, then I will be staying," said the grateful visitor.

"James, dear," said my mother. "After dinner, please get the bedroll down from the attic for our weary friend to sleep upon."

After the dishes were cleaned, my mother soon fell asleep upon the couch next to the fireplace. Tim Dronner and I spoke of many things, but more often than not the topic turned to whaling.

"Why don't we look for a ship that would suit us both, Master Jim? New Bedford has plenty of tall ships."

"What? You are not thinking of getting me to join you on some absurd voyage to fight whales, Tim?"

"The thought had crossed my mind," he responded, "seeing as how we have become fast friends. Don't answer now, Jim, sleep on it and we can talk again in the morning."

CHAPTER 3

An Offer from Captain Flynn

The next morning dawned brightly as I awoke to the sound of seagulls flying overhead. My new friend, Tim, and my mother were putting something together for breakfast in the kitchen. As I walked in, the two were jabbering as if they had known each other for years.

"What are you two talking about?" I asked.

"Wouldn't you like to know," responded my mother slyly.

"I think I can guess, dear woman," was my reply. "Our old friend Tim here has been filling your head with wild stories about how he and I are bound to be shipmates on a Yankee whaler."

"How would it be that you could know such things," asked my mother. "You never used to be able to listen through walls."

Turning my attention to the overzealous visitor, I quipped, "Give up this foolishness, lad. You are only bound to upset my fragile mother's constitution. Besides, we had best turn our attention to the more urgent need of finding you employment. Even whale men need money to live on, and you have the need to buy a load of gear before you think about setting foot on a bark."

"Very well," agreed the slender country boy, reluctantly.

After completing a brief but satisfying breakfast, Tim and I hitched a ride on a horse drawn wagon that was headed for town. As the minutes passed by we discussed how and where we would try to find him work.

"How do you earn a living?" asked Tim.

"For years now," I answered, "I have found work doing odd

jobs for almost every shopkeeper in town. If you have a mind for work and a strong back, someone will at least give you day wages running errands or working on the wharfs unloading cargo."

Tim smiled widely for several moments, and then, amidst chuckles, stated that he was not so sure if he wanted to work for the blacksmith.

"He is a might too stern for my liking," concluded Tim.

"His bark is worse than his bite," I added with a smile. "Besides, he is not the only blacksmith in New Bedford."

A few minutes later, the tiny cart came to an abrupt halt at the outskirts of town.

"This is where ye lads must depart," shouted the driver. "I hope you earn a few dollars for your sweat this day."

As we jumped from the back of the cart, Tim tossed the driver a hard biscuit and put his floppy hat on more securely.

"Now where?" asked Tim.

"Straight ahead to the wharf," I asserted. "Just follow the gulls. Two vessels are due in today so we should be able to find some kind of work."

Several minutes passed before we reached the vicinity of the wharf. As predicted, the entire area around the docks was a beehive of activity. As I knew the routine, I took the initiative to inquire with the manager of the docks about the availability of work.

The dock foreman was a wiry chap by the name of Terry. He sported a large mustache and a huge scar on the side of his face. The scar was a momento from his younger days as a pirate, I was told.

"Who is it that ye brought with you, Jim boy?" inquired the scarred man.

"My friend's name is Timothy, Timothy Dronner sir," I answered.

"Can he work, Jim?" questioned the foreman. "He looks

much too pretty to be a working man. We don't hire no green-horns, Jim boy."

"I can work well enough," said Tim. "Give me a chance to prove myself."

"He speaks pretty bold for a lad with no references," barked the foreman. "Oh, well, I am in a tight spot today so I will try him out for size just this once."

Something like a smile broke out on Tim's face as he followed the dock manager over to where his first job was to begin.

As the sun rose higher in the sky, Tim and I unloaded cargo of every sort. The afternoon's work dragged on as we endured the incessant rambling of the foreman who yelled, "Put your backs into it, boys!" at least a hundred times. The best part of the day, by far, was the lunch break. We were permitted to eat our fish and chips in relative peace as we took turns feeding the seagulls with our scraps.

Strange smells also intruded themselves upon us during our labors on the wharf next to Water Street. Among the more memorable smells was the scent of whale oil mixed with dried fish. My friend, Tim, had a particularly difficult time handling the peculiar and sometimes overpowering odors. More than once, my friend from the country seemed to turn a strange shade of green as he struggled to adapt to the rude smells.

A man had to work hard to earn two dollars a day in the 1840s, but we were glad to have the work just the same. Our day work down at the wharf lasted six days before the foreman ran short of work.

A new week began and my friend and I were, once again, in search of employment. We eventually landed work running errands for the local baker, which involved transporting barrels of bread from his shop to the holds of several vessels being outfitted for their eventual voyage.

I still remember how it felt when we first set foot on a whaling ship. All was clean and tidy on board as a rule, and the sheer size of the masts and yardarm were enough to impress most persons our age.

The wealthier ship owners had their whaling vessels trimmed with fixtures made of brass or whalebone. Some of the whalers that had captured whales in previous voyages also utilized the jawbones of their victims to form a portion of the rudder shafts or helms.

Late one day, as we were finishing up a delivery of hardtack to a three-masted schooner, we received an important message from the baker. His message told us of an urgent delivery that needed to be made before nightfall.

The most famous captain in New Bedford town, Captain Argus Flynn, was set to sail within a fortnight, and he was anxious to get his supplies safely stored in his ship's hold. Little did we know of how our lives would change as a result of a simple delivery of hard biscuits.

Captain Flynn's vessel, the *Landsman,* was well known to the citizens of New Bedford, so we had little trouble finding his ship. As the cart we were driving pulled alongside the ivory-trimmed *Landsman,* a skinny man in a broad-rimmed hat called to us saying, "Ahoy there, what's your business, lads?" We informed the strange looking sailor of our mission, and he quickly motioned for us to haul our cargo up the gangplank, and then disappeared. Moments later, we began to carry ten barrels onto the main deck of the *Landsman* with the assistance of heavy leather straps. All during this process, much to our surprise, we saw nary a soul. We suspected that the man who greeted us had gone below deck and that we were free to go.

We no sooner turned around, however, before we were staring directly at none other than Captain Flynn himself.

"Well, well, what brings ye landlubbers aboard my ship?" questioned the captain. "Has the baker finally gotten 'round to making good on my order of hardtack?"

"Yea, sir," I responded. "Ten barrels, just as you ordered, Captain."

"How would you like to earn an extra half dollar in silver this fine evening?" asked Captain Flynn.

Tim responded, "We ain't afraid of hard work, and anyways, we could sure use the extra pay, for we're fixing to outfit ourselves as whalers."

"Oh, whale men, shipmates is it then!" said the captain. "Well, why don't you ambitious lads show me what you're made of by stowing these here barrels below deck, as well as the others over yonder."

The captain excused himself, and we set to work clearing the deck of cargo and storing it in the hold below. Several minutes later, after we had finished our main task, the first mate directed us to help him stow surplus canvas in a special place in the forecastle of the *Landsman*.

"She sure is a fine ship," said Tim admiringly as we prepared to leave.

Captain Flynn had overheard my friend Tim and said, "I can see you are a good judge of vessels, lad, even if you are a mite bit green. Here be your half dollar."

"Thank you, sir," said I. "Will you be needin' anything else, Captain, before we shove off?"

"No more to do at this hour," said the captain slowly as he stroked his cropped beard. "All I ask is that you help spread the word that the *Landsman* needs several new mates, for five of my regular crew have taken sick of late and likely will be unfit to sail."

"Might we qualify as shipmates, sir?" said Tim impulsively.

"What do you mean by we, friend? I don't recall Jim Surrey ever committing to be a whaler," said I.

"Hold onto your hats, lads," recommended Captain Flynn. "I know you both are hard working souls, but what else can ye do besides stow cargo? Can either of ye sing and hold to a cadence? Can ye pull teeth or set an arm, or do anything useful as a mate?"

"Well, sir, I mean, Captain," mumbled Tim. "My father taught me many things on the farm, including how to pull the teeth of animals and how to set the broken leg of a sheep."

"Excellent!" yelled the captain. "You will do nicely as our ship's doctor. Now what about your reluctant shipmate?"

"My reluctance to sign on, sir, has to do with the death of my father these three years ago," said I. "Even now, my dear widowed mother is barely making it by with my help. As for singing, my father was a whaler and a hearty singer, and he taught me all the songs of the chanteyman."

"My regrets, son, on the loss of your father, but may you not do your mother more financial good by earning profits as a whale man rather than an errand boy?"

"Perhaps," said I. "But I doubt that I would do my mother any service by leaving her alone for three years."

"Rest easy, son, for my ship is outward bound for only a two-year voyage," added the captain. "Furthermore, you can perhaps find someone to care for your mother in your absence. Think on it well, lad, and let me know your decision soon."

As Tim and I walked down the gangplank to the waiting horse and cart, we barely said a word. Each of us was lost in his own thoughts.

Finally, after a minute or two, Tim asked, "Am I dreaming, or did Captain Argus Flynn just hire me on as a mate and ship's doctor?"

"I'm afraid so," I responded. "It should be a wild adventure for you and for your patients, doctor."

"Jim, don't think for a moment that I would go to sea without you. If you refuse to go then my answer to the captain will also be 'no'."

CHAPTER 4

The Seaman's Bethel

The thought of seeking approval from my widow mother for a two-year voyage was only slightly less distasteful than the notion of continuing on in the role of an errand boy indefinitely.

Several days had already gone by, however, since I spoke with Captain Flynn and time was growing short. Therefore, I determined to approach my mother and let her know my desires. At midweek, I decided to come home early so as to be able to speak with her.

"Good evening, Mother," was my greeting.

"My word, is it evening already, Son, or has my sense of time gone away?" she responded.

"Your senses are still with you, Mother. I decided to come home early so we could talk."

"What's on your mind, Son? You look perplexed."

"I am," said I. "Captain Argus Flynn has asked Timothy and me to sign on his crew for a two-year voyage. He says that it is just the break a young man like me needs."

"Oh, I see," responded my mother softly. "And what, if I may ask, will happen with me?"

"That's why I am perplexed, Mother," I said frankly.

"When I don't know how to figure out things, I call on Reverend Carlson down at the Seaman's Bethel for counsel," asserted my mother. "Why don't you pay him a visit this very night?"

"I haven't been very regular at services lately, Mother, with my long hours at work. Do you think he will see me?"

"Yes, Son. Now go get washed up and see if you can borrow the neighbor's horse for your ride to New Bedford."

Thanks to the generosity of our next-door neighbor, I was soon on my way to visit the parson who lived atop Johnnycake Hill.

The Seaman's Bethel had been the primary church for whale men in New Bedford town since my father was in britches. Any sailor with an ounce of spiritual concern would pay a visit to the Bethel prior to departing on a voyage, so as to make peace with his Maker. The church building itself, which had held many a whaler's wedding and funeral, was decorated with plaques that commemorated the voyages and deaths of many sailors.

As I began to approach the vicinity of the church, I passed numerous small ships and boarding houses. Moving down the cobbled streets on horseback was more difficult than I had anticipated, so I decided to dismount and walk the final block to Rev. Carlson's parsonage.

Upon arriving, I knocked on the front door of the tiny dwelling. Moments later, I heard footsteps and was soon standing before the venerable preacher. He invited me into his study after I explained the purpose of my visit, and we set to talking.

"So how is your dear mother these days, James?" questioned the minister.

"Very well, Reverend."

"How can I be of service to you this evening?" he asked.

"I need your advice on a matter that concerns my mother and my career. It all stems from the fact that, only recently, I've been offered a spot on Captain Flynn's crew and must quickly decide whether to leave my mother to further my career."

"I see," said the parson. "And you are wondering whether it is right to place the demands of your vocation above the needs of your widowed mother."

"Yes, I suppose that is what it amounts to, sir."

"Our Lord had a critically important job to do in His capacity as Savior, a work which placed Him in the position of having to leave His beloved mother. Yet, the Scriptures tell us that Christ took the time to ensure that Mary would be well cared for after His departure. As Jesus hung on the cross, He made sure to entrust His mother's care into the hands of John, a trusted friend."

"And you are saying, then, that I should seek to do no less? Is that correct?"

"Yes, precisely, my friend," said Rev. Carlson.

"Do you have any recommendations for a suitable caretaker for my mother?" I asked.

"Yes, I have but one recommendation, dear lad, me."

"Forgive me preacher, but I thought I just heard you say that you would care for my mother for the next two years."

"Your hearing is quite intact, James," responded the preacher with a smile.

"I— I hardly know what to say except 'Thank you,' and that I will pledge to help you pay for my mother's care upon my return."

"I know you will do what you can out of your limited means, James," Rev. Carlson assured me. "Now promise me that you will be at the Sunday service before you ship out."

"Very well, Reverend. Thanks again for your help."

We closed our meeting a short time later, as the evening was drawing fast on. As I began my homeward journey, my thoughts quickly passed into how my mother would react to the unexpected proposal.

Much to my surprise, my mother was rather at peace with the notion of Rev. Carlson as her temporary guardian. She obviously believed that she would be well looked after, because she knew that the preacher was a man of his word.

When I broke the news to Tim Dronner about my acceptance of Captain Flynn's invitation to join his crew, I thought he would come unglued. Shouts of joy and something like an Irish jig quickly sprung forth from us both, much to the amusement of onlookers.

Our momentary glee soon turned more to sober contemplation, however, as we both considered how ill-equipped we were to take to sea. With only three days left before our departure, my shipmate and I decided to pay a visit to the outfitters and clothing shops on Main Street.

Our inexperience forced us to ask the proprietor of the best clothing shop in town what gear he would recommend that whalers purchase. As Tim and I listened carefully, the shop owner gave us our first lesson on seafaring survival.

"Cold, wet, and dirty work it is, boys," began the shopkeeper. "I urge you to obtain two heavy wool sweaters, a good pair of waterproof boots, and above all else a set of oilskins. O yes, and for your sakes, and that of your shipmates, don't forget to bring plenty of soap!"

Within one hour, much to our satisfaction, we had purchased nearly all the gear we needed, and certainly all we could afford. The advice we received was worth its weight in gold, and many times at sea we were thankful to God and the shopkeeper for their help.

The time was fast approaching when we would need to board the *Landsman,* and we soon began to say our good-byes in town and at home. The day before we were to depart was Sunday, the Lord's day, so I finished the last of my errands on Saturday and prepared to attend the Seaman's Bethel service as promised. Although it took a bit of prodding, I was able to convince Tim Dronner to join me for the worship service on Sunday morning, as well.

The church meeting that Sunday was unusually crowded as sailors from all over the area were intent on getting right with the Almighty before they began a dangerous voyage. Precisely at eleven o'clock, Rev. Carlson emerged from his study to take the pulpit.

He opened, "Beloved friends and shipmates, let us pray. Almighty God, who hears prayers that are offered up in spirit and in truth, unite our hearts in the holy exercise of biblical worship. Permit us to feed upon Your Word and Spirit to the nourishment of our needy souls. Grant that we may enter into Your rest and Your peace this day through Jesus Christ our Lord. Amen."

"For many of you," the preacher continued, "this Lord's day marks your last time of fellowship with us, for you will soon be shipping out and unable to attend sacred worship here for an extended period of time. For at least a few of you, however, this may well be the last time you ever visit the Seaman's Chapel because you will have tasted death and been ushered into the presence of your Maker. The question is, shipmates, are you prepared for what the Lord brings into your path? Can you say, with the Apostle Paul, 'For me to live is Christ and to die is gain'?"

"My primary message to you today comes from the book of First Timothy, chapter one. In this passage, Paul the Apostle acknowledges that before Christ took over his life, he was a blasphemer, a persecutor of Christians, and a violent man. All men sailing through the journey of life, like Paul, are sinners and are unworthy of the love and grace of God.

"Beloved friends, have you ever been brought to the place of seeing yourself as Paul saw himself? As one who is totally unfit for heaven? If so, then you have discovered a truth that will lead you to a Rock that is higher than yourself; you will have seen your need for an anchor for your souls. Hope then will be near, as near as the Savior Jesus Christ is to His lost sheep. As David the Psalmist declared in Psalm Thirty-Four, verse eighteen, 'The Lord is nigh unto them that are of a broken heart; and saveth such as be of a contrite spirit.' Will you abandon your proud spirit to receive the free offer of mercy and grace that God's Word offers you today? Will you accept, by faith, the bloody work of Christ on Calvary's cross as the full atonement for your sins?

"Dear ones, you must answer these questions with a willing mind or perish! You must come to God, through the mercy of Christ alone, by faith alone, and by the power of the Holy Spirit alone. Should your hard, stony hearts cast away the words of this Gospel of Christ, mark me well, ye having cast off faith will surely make shipwreck. This truth is made plain by Paul the Apostle in First Timothy, chapter one, verse nineteen.

"Think on these things well, shipmates, and pray for the Lord to grant you the gifts of faith and repentance, without which no one will gain peace and joy in this life or in the next. Amen."

Rev. Carlson concluded the service with the hymn *Amazing Grace,* which was written by a former sea captain and slave trader, John Newton. After the final hymn, many of the men stayed in the church sanctuary for several minutes and said the last of their farewells to family and friends.

The following morning, I went early to the ship after a tearful parting with my mother. As it was still early spring, I was grateful that I had remembered to put on my thickest sweater, for the air was cool. Looking across the docks, I noticed the familiar face of my friend and shipmate, Tim, as he approached.

In keeping with an old custom, we both kneeled down and kissed the ground before making our way on to the *Landsman.* As we approached the gangplank, I turned to my friend and said, "After you, Doctor Dronner, my esteemed colleague."

"Get off it, Jim," moaned my agitated friend as he chased me up the gangplank and onto the ship.

CHAPTER 5

Under Sail at Last

The breeze quickened as the crew of the *Landsman* made final preparations for setting sail out of the harbor. As the stoutest men stepped forward to work together to hoist the anchor, the first mate called out to me.

"Chanteyman, give these hearties something to pull to, a song lad, a song!"

As the men began to pull in unison, I opened my mouth and chanted this verse of song: "O boats and clothes are all in port."

The chorus was then immediately sung by the workingmen in unison, "Go round your blood red roses, go round. Oh, your pinks and posies; Go round your blood red roses, go round."

Then I sang, "For it's round Cape Horn that we must go," before the men chimed in with another repeat of the chorus.

And my chantey continued, "For that is where them whale fish blow."

On and on my chantey song went as I added one new verse at a time, while the response of the crew was always to repeat the simple chorus in unison.

The job of the chanteyman was, more than anything, to keep the morale of the men high as they frequently faced difficult and demanding physical labor. As even a landlover can recognize, hard tasks seem a bit lighter and more pleasant when they are done to music.

In what seemed like no time, the anchor was hoisted and we heard the captain yell, "Put on every inch of canvas she will hold, aloft I say!"

The *Landsman* came to life with the assistance of fresh breezes as it glided smoothly out of the harbor into the open sea. Before long, the tiny buildings of New Bedford town were just a memory. We were, at last, enjoying the opening of our high sea adventure with all of its great expectations.

The initial exuber-
ance of sailors such as
myself quickly
faded, how-
ever, as the
rolling
waves
o f

the ocean became more angry. My first few days on the ocean were so miserable that I oftentimes repented from having left my native land. I was, as my new friend Tim Dronner said, "As sick as a dog." In course of time, however, I overcame the sickness and began to get my "sealegs" as sailors put it.

Whenever time permitted, and the weather was calm, I used to creep out to the end of the bowsprit, and sit with my legs dangling over the deep blue water and my eyes fixed on the rolling clouds, thinking of the new direction I had taken in my life. At such times, the thought of my mother would often come to mind and I would remember her parting words, "Put your trust in the Lord, James, and read His Word."

I resolved to try to obey her, but I found that this was no easy matter, for most of my shipmates cared little for the Bible. Still, I was blest with a few mates to help keep me on the straight and narrow. On the whole, I must say, that the vast majority of the crew was even-tempered and much better in character than many a ship's crew that I afterward endured.

Our first weeks at sea went rather smoothly as the men became accustomed to working with the captain and the ship. Fair winds blew us gracefully onward toward our first destination, which was the whaling grounds of the South Atlantic. Soon we found ourselves on the other side of "the line", as we sailors call the equator.

As we crossed over the equator, the seasoned crewmembers enacted an old custom of shaving the heads of all the men who had never crossed the line before. Needless to say, Tim and I wore caps quite regularly for several days, as the mates employed in the shaving were poor barbers indeed!

In between seasons of hard work and silly games or customs, there was general boredom on board. I tried my best, through the use of music, to minimize these periods of tedious boredom. As long as the men did not engage in fighting or destructive behavior, Captain Flynn gave them leave to do what they liked during their free time.

To keep from going insane, many men had a hobby or craft that they practiced in their spare time. The most popular hobby on the *Landsman,* as it was on most whalers, involved the carving of images or decorations onto the face of the bones or teeth of whales. This craft, which is truly an art form, is called "scrimshaw." Sailors would work hour after hour, sitting and scratching on the surface of the whale bones while they patiently filled their designs with ink.

It was already well into the month of May, and although our voyage out was relatively trouble free, we were all getting anxious to spot our first whale. At last, we arrived at our hunting ground in the South Seas, and a feeling of excitement began to show on the faces of the crew. When the expectation for battle begins to flow in the veins of the men, the old-timers refer to it as the time when "the blood is up."

One night, those of us who had just been relieved from watch on deck were sitting on the lockers down below, telling stories about monstrous whales. It was dead calm, and one of those intensely dark, hot nights that cause sailors to feel uneasy without any reason. Right in the middle of a story about a giant man-eating whale by the name of "Big Tom," I stopped the storyteller and asked a question. "Tell me truly, mate, can a whale really sink ships and eat men alive?"

"My young shipmate," began the man, "whales can do almost anything. They can rise up like a mountain and crash down like thunder. They can stay at the bottom of the ocean for over an hour, then rise and swim faster than a bark. One little flick of its tail can turn several long boats into splinters and wives into widows. Yes, laddie, whales can do monstrous things."

I noticed that these scary stories were beginning to get to Tim Dronner as I watched him move quietly toward the ladder leading up from the forecastle. Just as Tim had ascended the ladder and was almost topside, he turned to listen to the blood-chilling ending to the story. Moments later, I watched as Tim became so nervous that he lost his sense of balance, slipped and fell down right in among the men. A loud crash and a hearty yell could be heard throughout most of the ship as Tim managed to knock over two or three oilcans and a tin basket full of bread in his fall.

The room fell instantly dark, and soon you could hear a symphony of howls and screams coming from the darkened room. Men in various stages of panic began to emerge from the forecastle onto the main deck, only to be greeted by the laughter of the crew on watch. The fresh air and smiles soon caused the traumatized evacuees to recognize their folly and to join in the laughter. I noticed, however, that for all their pretended indifference, there was not one man among them who had the courage to go down below to relight the lanterns for over an hour.

Shortly after this unusual turn of events, I went forward and leaned over the bow of the ship. I was astonished by the appearance of the water that night. It seemed as if the sea was on fire! Every time the ship's bow rose and fell, the little belt of foam made in the water seemed like a blue flame with bright sparks, like stars or diamonds. I had seen this curious sight before, but never so bright as it was that night.

"What is this bright blue flame in the ocean?" said I, as the captain was passing by.

"It is caused by small animals," he said, leaning over the side.

"Small animals!" I repeated, in astonishment.

"Aye, many parts of the sea are full of creatures so small and so thin and colorless that you can hardly see them even in a clear glass tumbler. A few of them are somewhat large, but most of them are very small."

"But how do they shine like that, sir?" I asked.

"That I do not know, boy. God has given them the power to shine, just as He has given us the power to speak or walk. As you can see, there is no denying that they shine, but how they do it is more than I can tell. I think, myself, it must be anger that makes them shine, for they generally do it when they are stirred up or knocked about by oars, or ships' keels. But I am not sure that that's the reason either because, you know, we often sail through them without seeing the light, though, of course, they must be there."

"Perhaps, sir," I added, "perhaps they're sleepy sometimes, an' can't be bothered getting angry."

"I never thought of it that way," answered Captain Flynn, laughing. "But, on the other hand, I have seen them shining over the whole sea when it was quite calm, making it like an ocean of cream. Nothing seemed to be bothering them at that time, if ye know what I mean."

"Oh, I can't be sure of that," I objected. "They might have been fightin' among themselves, or maybe playing."

Argus Flynn smiled widely and, looking up at the sky, said, "I don't like the look of the weather, chanteyman."

"We'll have a strong breeze," I replied briefly.

"More than a breeze, my dull friend," muttered the captain, while a look of anxiety began to fill his face; "I'll go below and take a squint at the glass."

As Captain Flynn was heading off, my friend, Tim Dronner, who overheard his parting comments, asked, "What does the captain mean by that, Jim? I never saw a calmer or a finer night. Surely there is no chance of a storm just now."

"Well, I am not sure what to make of it," I responded. "Perhaps the first mate, Mr. Owens, will have an answer."

Tim and I walked over to the starboard side of the ship and found the first mate looking up at the sky intently. "What do ye make of this evening's weather?" I asked. "We can't figure out why the captain is so jumpy on such a fine night as this."

"Aye, that shows that you're a young mate and lack the experience to judge the sky and seas," replied Owens. "Why, lad, sometimes the fiercest storm is brewin' behind the greatest calm. And the worst of things is that it comes so sudden at times that the masts are torn out of the ship before you can say 'Jack Robinson'."

"I thought the only warning a sailor needed was in the sky during the night or early morning," asserted my friend, Tim. "Ye know the old saying, sir, 'Red sky in the morning, sailor's warning; Pink sky at night, sailor's delight'."

"Ye are a green one at that," said the first mate. "Many a storm brews at sea almost without warnin', but not altogether without it.

If I know anything about our captain and the sea, I'd wager that he was, even now, taking a hard look at the glass."

"Tell us, Mr. Owens, what is the glass?"

"It's not a glass o' grog, you may be certain; nor yet a lookin'-glass. It's the weather-glass, boy. Shore-goin' landlubbers call it a barometer."

"How does a barometer work?" Tim asked.

"Mate," responded Owens, "Ye are too full of questions, but I will answer this one as best I can. A barometer is a glass tube filled with quicksilver, or mercury, which is a metal in a soft or fluid state, like water, and it changes with the weather. The barometer somehow measures the weight of the air and lets you know what's coming. If the mercury in the glass rises high, all is well. If it falls suddenly very low, look out for squalls. No matter how smooth the sea may be, or how sweetly all nature may smile, don't you believe it; take in every inch of canvas at once."

As I looked upon the calm sea, which lay like a sheet of glass, without a ripple on its surface, I could scarcely believe what Mr. Owens had said. But, before many minutes had passed, I was convinced of my error.

While I was standing talking to my friend, the ship's doctor, the captain rushed on deck, and shouted: "All hands, tumble up! Shorten sail! Take in every rag! Look alive, boys; Step lively!"

I was quite stunned for a moment by this, and by the sudden commotion that followed. The men, who rarely seemed to be in a hurry, sprang to their duty and obeyed the order of their captain without hesitation.

Before long, the deck was full of men, some of whom leaped up the rigging like cats. The sheets of nearly all the principal sails were clewed up, and ere long the canvas was made fast to the yards. Only a few of the smaller sails were left exposed, and even these were close-reefed.

A short time later, a loud roar was heard, and in another minute, the storm burst upon us with terrific force. The ship was tossed violently to its side so that the yards were almost in the water, and it immediately became impossible for anyone to walk the deck, for it was like walking on the side of a wall. At the same moment, the sea was stirred into white foam and the blinding spray flew over us in bitter fury.

"Take in the topsails!" roared the captain. But his voice was all but drowned in the shriek of the gale. The men were saved the risk of going out on the yards, however, for in a few moments more, all the sails except the storm-try-sail were burst and blown to ribbons.

The helmsman was then ordered to put the ship's head to the wind and "lay to," by which landlubbers will understand that we tried to face the storm and remain stationary. But the gale was so fierce that this was impossible. The last rag of sail was blown away, and then there was nothing left for us but to show our stern to the gale, and "scud under bare poles."

The great danger now was that we might be "pooped," which means that a huge wave might curl over our stern, fall with a terrible fury on our deck, and sink us. Many a good ship and crew had gone down in this way; but we were mercifully spared by the Almighty.

The captain himself decided to take the ship's wheel, since safety largely depended upon good steering. He managed the ship so well that we weathered the storm without much damage, save a few sails and spars. For two whole days, the storm howled and the sea and sky were like ink. Raging billows tossed our ship about like a cork as the air was saturated with white foam and sheets of rain.

During all this time, my shipmates were quiet and serious, as well as diligent and full of energy, so that every order was at once obeyed without murmuring. Everyone on board knew that we were in great danger, and that we were close to meeting our Maker.

As for me, I had all but given up hope of being saved. It seemed impossible to me that anything that man could build could withstand so terrible a storm. I will not pretend to say that I was not afraid. The near prospect of a violent death caused my heart to sink more than once; but my feelings of helplessness did not destroy my manhood or dignity. I did my duty quietly and quickly, like the rest; and when I had no work to do, I stood holding on to the weather stanchions, looking at the angry sea, and thinking of my mother, and of the words of kindness and counsel she had so often bestowed upon me in vain.

After what seemed like a week, the storm ceased almost as quickly as it began. As the breeze began to slacken, the dark clouds broke up into great masses that were piled high in the sky. Out of the midst of the clouds the glorious sun shone in bright rays down on the ocean, like comfort from heaven, gladdening our hearts as we busily repaired the damage done to the ship from the storm.

CHAPTER 6
There She Blows!

I shall never forget the thrill I got the first time I saw a whale at sea. It was in the forenoon of a most splendid day, about a week after we arrived at that part of the ocean where we might expect to find whales. A light nor' east breeze was blowing, but it scarcely ruffled the sea, as we crept slowly through the water with every stitch of canvas set.

Due to the fact that we had been looking out for whales for several days, everything was in readiness for them. The boats were hanging over the side, ready to lower. The tubs for coiling away the rope as well as the harpoons, lances, and so forth were also ready to throw in and start away at a moment's notice. The man in the "crow's nest"—as they call the small platform located at the top of the mast-head—was busy looking out for whales while the crew was anxiously pacing the deck below.

During this time, my shipmate, the doctor, was attending to one of his first patients, who needed to have a fresh bandage placed upon his head. It seems as though this mate managed to knock his head into one of the masts during the confusion and tempest of the preceding days' storm. Doctor Tim was seated on the windlass, finishing up his first aid duty, while I was sitting near him on an empty barrel, sharpening a blubber-knife and practicing a new chantey.

I turned slowly toward my shipmate and muttered, "When on Earth are we going to see a living, breathing whale? If all these stories about monstrous whales are true, why can't we spot them?"

Doctor Tim reminded me that whales can't be spotted well at night and then added, "Besides, these big creatures like to swim far and deep. Many big whales can travel the whole world round in only twenty days. The captain himself told me just yesterday that whales are constantly on the move."

The only response I gave to this explanation was to shrug my shoulders. Shortly thereafter, however, the silence was broken by the sailor perched in the crow's nest as he roared at the top of his voice, "There she blows!"

For the first time that season, the signal that a whale was in sight was heard. Every man on board the *Landsman* was thrown into a state of tremendous excitement.

"There she blows!" roared the lookout again.

"Where away?" shouted Captain Flynn.

"About two miles dead ahead," came the response.

The entire crew sprang to life as they gathered the tools of their trade in anticipation of the captain's orders. At the same time, the first mate ordered the sails to be taken in or shortened. As the ship began to slow down and settle deeper in the water, I ran over to the starboard side of the ship. Moments later, while I was looking over the side, straining my eyes to catch a sight of the whale, which could not as yet be seen by the sailors on deck, I saw a dark gray object appear in the sea not twenty yards from the side of the *Landsman*. Before I had time to identify the strange creature, a whale's head rose to the surface and shot up out of the water. The part of the creature that was visible above the water could not have been less than thirty feet in length. He was so near that I could see his great mouth quite plainly and could have tossed a biscuit in between his massive teeth had I possessed the courage.

The dark gray giant sent two thick spouts of frothy water out of his blowholes forty feet into the air with a tremendous noise. He then fell flat upon the sea with a clap that sounded like thunder, tossed his flukes, or tail, high into the air, and disappeared.

I was so amazed by this sight that I could not speak. I could only manage to stare and point at the place where the huge monster had gone down.

"Stand by to lower!" shouted the captain.

"Aye, aye, sir," replied the men, leaping to their appointed stations. Every man on a whaling ship, I would tell you, had his post of duty appointed to him and was responsible to know what to do when an order was given.

"Lower away!" cried Argus Flynn, whose face was now an interesting shade of red and full of excitement.

Within two minutes, three long boats were in the water, each with a crew of six men. The captain himself guided one vessel as the headsman, and the other two boats were directed by the first and second mates. As soon as the tubs and harpoons were secured, the men seized the oars and pulled hard in the direction the headsman signaled.

I was in such a state of excitement that I hardly knew what I was doing. Somehow or other, I managed to get into a boat; and, as I was a strong fellow and a good rower, I was quickly put to work.

"There she blows!" cried the man, one last time, just as we moved away from the ship. There was no need to ask, "Where away?" this time. Another whale soon rose and spouted not more than three hundred yards off. Before we could speak, a third creature rose in another direction, and we found ourselves in the middle of what is called a "school of whales."

Harpoons

"Now, lads," said the captain, as he steered the boat in which I rowed, "bend your backs, my hearties. That creature straight ahead of us is a hundred-barrel whale for certain. Give way, boys; pull I say! We must have that fish!"

There was no need to urge the men, for their blood was up and their backs were strained to the utmost. My face, and that of the other sailors, was flushed. I felt as though the big veins in my neck were swelled almost to bursting with the tremendous exertion.

"Hold hard," said the captain, in a low voice, for now that we were getting near our prey we made as little noise as possible. "Oars a peak," continued our leader, as we raised our oars straight up in the air, and awaited further orders.

We expected that the whale would sound near to where we were, and thought it best to rest and look out for where the creature may rise. I then noticed that the other boats had separated, and each had gone after a different whale. After a few minutes the whale we were chasing rose a short distance off and sent two splendid waterspouts high into the air, thus showing that he was what whalers call a "right" whale. It is different from the sperm whale, which has only one blowhole and a longer, leaner head.

We rowed toward it with all our might, and as we drew near the captain ordered, "Harpooner! Stand up! Stand by your iron!"

The harpooner made his way to the bow of the whaleboat and balanced himself on a small platform positioned there. In his hand was a long iron shaft with a barbed point that had a rope attached to it, which was coiled away in a metal tub nearby.

When we were within a few yards of the whale, which was going through the water, unaware of the dangerous foes who were pursuing him, Captain Flynn shouted, "Give it to him!"

The harpooner raised the weapon high above his head and darted it deep into the monster's side just behind his left fin.

"Give him the lance!" ordered the leader.

Immediately after the second weapon reached its mark, the headsman ordered the crew to back the boat away from the thrashing whale.

"Stern all! Stern all, row for your lives!" roared the captain, as the boat was dangerously close to running aground on the whale's back.

While we were backing away from the heaving monster, Captain Flynn managed to give the creature one deep wound with his lance. The lance has no barbs to its point and is used only for wounding after the harpoon is fixed.

Our boat was backed off at once, but it had scarcely moved a few yards away before the astonished creature whirled its huge body half out of the water and, coming down with a loud clap, made off like lightning.

The line that held the whale passed through a strong piece of wood called the "logger-head," and as the giant mammal began to run, the rope began to smoke and nearly set the wood on fire. Indeed, it would have done so, if a man had not kept water pouring down upon it. It was necessary for the sailor who was responsible for managing the line to be very cautious, for the dangers involved were extreme. If anything went wrong with the line so that it would get caught on the boat, it would likely drag both the boat and crew under the waves. On certain occasions, a coil of rope gets caught around a leg or an arm of a man who attends to it, in which case he is almost certain to lose life or a limb. Many a poor sailor has lost his life in just this way.

The order was given by Argus Flynn to "hold on line." This was done, and in a moment our boat was clearing the blue water like an arrow, while the white foam curled from her bow. Every moment, I fully expected that we would be dragged under, but whenever this seemed likely to happen the line was let run a bit, and the strain eased. At last, the giant creature grew tired of dragging us and the line ceased to run out. One of our men hauled in the slack, and another mate coiled the rope away in its storage tub. Several moments later, the right whale rose to the surface, a short distance off our weather-bow.

"Give way, boys! Spring your oars!" cried the captain. "Another touch or two with the lance and that giant is ours."

Our boat shot ahead as the whale began to pick up speed once again. Just as our leader was about to dart another harpoon into the whale's side, it took to "sounding"—which means that it went straight down, head first, into the depths of the sea.

At that moment, Captain Flynn uttered a cry mingled with anger and disappointment. We all turned round and saw our shipmate standing with the slack line in his hand, and such an expression on his weather-beaten face as to make it hard not to laugh. The original harpoon had apparently not been well fixed and had lost its hold. The mighty giant was free once again!

"Gone!" exclaimed the captain with a groan.

Even now, I yet remember the awful feeling of disappointment that came over me when I understood that we had lost the whale after all our trouble. As for my comrades, they sat staring at each other for some time without saying a word. Before we could all recover from this frustrating incident, one of the men suddenly shouted, "Hello! There's the mate's boat in distress."

We turned at once, and truly, there was no doubt of the truth of this, for about half a mile off we beheld our first mate's boat tearing over the sea like a sleek steamer. The vessel was enduring a treacherous "Nantucket sleighride" and two oars were set up on end, to signal our attention.

When a whale is struck fast, it sometimes happens that the whole of the line in a boat is run out. When this is about to occur, it becomes necessary to hold on as much as possible without running the boat under the water. In those cases of distress, an oar is set up on end to show that assistance is required, either from the ship or from the other boats. As the line comes closer and closer to its end, another oar is hoisted to signal that help must be sent quickly. If no assistance can be sent, the only thing that remains to be done is to cut the line and lose the prey. Whale men do anything in their power to avoid cutting a line, for the loss of a good harpoon, in addition to the whale itself, is very costly. For this reason, whalers are sometimes tempted to hold on to a dangerous ride a little too long.

When we saw, therefore, the mate's boat dashing away in this hazardous manner, we forgot our grief and determined to try to come to the aid of our comrades. We began to row toward them as fast as we could. In the providence of God, however, the whale changed its course and came straight toward us.

Moments later, our leader ordered us to cease pulling, and we waited for the uncooperative whale to come closer. As the other boat came on in our direction, we could see the foam curling up on her bow as she leaped and flew over the sea. I had trouble believing that wood and iron could bear such a strain. In a few minutes, they were almost abreast of us.

"You're holding too hard!" shouted the captain.

"Line is all out!" roared the mate in return.

Our comrades' boat was past almost before these short sentences could be spoken. But they had not gone more than twenty-five yards ahead of us, before the water rushed in over the bow, and the boat and crew were gone. Not a trace of them remained! The horror of that moment had not been fully felt, however, before the boat rose to the surface keel up. One after another, the heads of the sailors appeared. By God's grace, the line had broken under the strain, otherwise the entire crew probably would have gone to the bottom with her.

We instantly pulled them to safety, and were thankful to find that not a man was missing, though some were injured slightly and all were badly frightened. Our next task was to seek to right the capsized boat, an operation that was not accomplished without much labor and difficulty.

While we were busy helping our stranded mates, the third boat, which was under the charge of the second mate, had gone after the whale that had caused us so much trouble. When we had finished helping our capsized shipmates and began to look about us, we found that she was fast to the giant creature about a mile leeward.

"Hurrah, lads!" cried the captain. "Give way, my hearties, pull like vengeance! We'll get that big fish yet."

As tired as we all were by this point, only the sight of one of our boats tied fast to a whale restored our will to fight. We pulled away stoutly, then, as if we had only begun our day's work. The whale we were pursuing was heading in the general direction of the ship. When we came up to the final scene of action, the second mate had just "touched the life." In other words, he had driven the lance deep down into the whale's vitals. This was quickly known by the jets of blood being spouted up through the blowholes. Soon after, our victim went into its death roll, or as whale men say, "his flurry."

This did not last long, thankfully, for in a short time he rolled over dead. We quickly fastened lines to his head and tail, and then towed the carcass away to the ship.

While my job of hunting whales had almost come to a close that day, my job as a chanteyman had just begun. I sang out with a lively song known as "Heave Away Johnny", as my shipmates and I rowed our hard-fought treasure over to the *Landsman*.

Thus ended our first battle with big whales.

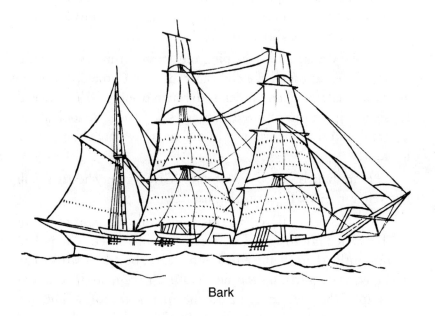

Bark

CHAPTER 7

A Floating Butcher Shop

The scene that took place on board ship after we caught our first whale was very interesting. Our initial task was, of course, to see to it that the right whale we caught was securely fastened to the *Landsman* with heavy chains. Then we began the operation of what is called "cutting in," that is, cutting up the whale and getting the fat or blubber hoisted aboard. The next thing we did was to "try out" the oil, or melt down the fat in large iron pots brought along for this purpose. In the final phase of our whale processing, we placed the oil in wooden barrels and cleaned up the ship.

The change that took place in the appearance of the ship and the men when this process began was very remarkable. When we left port our decks were clean, our sails white, and our masts well scraped and painted. Even the brass work around the quarterdeck was shiny and the men rather tidy and clean. A few hours after our first whale had been secured alongside, however, all this soon changed.

The cutting up of the huge carcass covered the decks with oil and blood, making them so slippery that they had to be covered with sand to enable the men to walk about. Then the smoke from the great fires under the huge melting pots soiled the masts, sails, and eventually the men. It soon became difficult to determine whether the crewmembers were white or black. Their clothes, too, became so dirty that it was impossible to clean them.

But it must be said that whale men, as a rule, did not much mind this dirty business. In fact, they often seemed to take pleasure in all the dirt that surrounded them, for they regarded it as a sign of success. The men in a clean whale ship were seldom happy. Only when all was filthy and dirty and greasy would you hear the sailors letting out a hearty laugh or a cheery song. Whale men worked hard, night and day, during such times but their labor was clearly profitable, so they could afford to smile.

The operations of cutting in and trying out were matters of great interest to me the first time I saw them. I will try my best to describe them more fully.

After having towed our whale to the ship and secured the head and tail with chains, we promptly attached a series of strong ropes and winches to the main and foremast. This equipment was used to hoist the huge pieces of blubber on board. In addition, our crew set up a long, narrow platform alongside the ship just above the whale. This platform was used by the men who were doing the cutting in.

I was stationed at one of the hoisting ropes during the cutting in stage. Shortly before our hoisting efforts began, I had an opportunity to peep over the side and take a good look at the size of the immense creature. This right whale was by no means a monstrous specimen; yet, due to the fact that it was the first whale I had seen, it seemed like it was one of the largest in the sea.

Its body was forty feet long and twenty feet round at the thickest part. Its head, which seemed to be a rounded, shapeless thing, was eight feet long from the tip to the blowholes or nostrils. These holes were situated on the back of its head. Its ears were two small holes and the eyes were also very small for so large a body, being about the same size as those of an ox. The right whale had a very large mouth, and its under jaw had huge ugly lips. It had two fins, one on each side, just behind the head.

The right whale swims and fights with its fins and tail. Its tail is its most deadly weapon. The flukes of the whale we caught measured thirteen feet across, and with one stroke of his tail he could have smashed our long boat in pieces. Many a whaleboat has been sent to the bottom of the sea as a result of getting hit by a whale's tail.

I remember hearing our first mate tell of a wonderful escape a comrade of his had in the North Atlantic. This friend was a harpooner, and was out chasing a whale one day. The men with which he was hunting rowed so hard that they ran their whaleboat right into the back of a whale. The harpooner was standing in position on the bow and sent his iron cleanly into the whale's side. In its agony, the whale reared its tail high out of the water, and the flukes whirred for a moment like a huge fan just above the harpooner's head. One glance up was enough to show him that certain death was descending. In an instant, he dove over the side and plunged into the cold sea. A moment later, the flukes came down on the point of the boat he had just left, and cut it clean off. The other part of the vessel was driven into the waves, and the men were left swimming in the water. They were all picked up, however, including the harpooner, by another boat that was in the hunting party. His quick dive had been the saving of his life.

I had only a short time given to me in which to study the appearance of the whale that was fastened to the *Landsman*. Before long, the order was given to "Hoist away!" so we went to work with a will. The first part that came up was the huge lip, fastened to a large iron hook, called the blubber-hook. It was lowered into the blubber-room between decks, where a couple of men were stationed to stow the blubber away. Then came the fins, and after them the upper jaw.

The job of cutting the whale into manageable chunks was essentially like the work of a butcher. Those who did the initial cutting stood on the cutting stage platform and hacked at the whale with long-handled, sharp spades or digging knives. They began by separating the head from the main body. The head was then sectioned into three parts. The top half of the head, or "case" contained the purest oil, which was often retrieved through the use of a bucket. The lower portion of the forehead, or "junk" yielded both spermaceti and oil. Spermaceti was fatty matter, which could be used to make ointments or candles. The remaining portion of the head contained the jaw and teeth, which were normally saved for scrimshaw or for trim on the ship.

Unlike the sperm whale, the right whale has no teeth. In place of teeth, it has the well-known substance called whalebone, or baleen, which grows from the roof of its mouth in a number of broad, thin plates. These plates extend from the back of the head to the snout. The lower edges of these plates of whalebone are split into thousands of hair-like bristles, so that the inside roof of the whale's mouth resembles an enormous brush! The bristles enable the whale to catch the little shrimps and small creel on which it feeds. When it desires a meal, it simply opens its large mouth and rushes into the midst of a school of tiny sea creatures. As soon as the whale has obtained a large enough mouthful, it shuts its lower jaw and swallows what its net has caught.

At any rate, let's get back to the story of our "cutting in" or flensing. After the upper jaw came the lower jaw with the tongue. The tongue was an enormous mass of fat, about as big as a large cow. Once the sections of the head were on board, the rest of the work was relatively simple. The work of cutting the blubber off in large strips or "blanket pieces" began at the neck as the body was peeled off in great strips in a spiral fashion ending at the tail. The massive blanket pieces were nearly a foot thick, and had the consistency of fatty pork.

As the blanket pieces were dropped into the blubber-room, two men were stationed there to cut it with knives into smaller "horse" pieces before being stored away. Then another huge strip was hoisted on board in the same fashion, and so on we went till every bit of blubber was cut off.

While our crew was busy processing its first whale, I noticed the arrival of a growing number of sea birds. I was soon informed of the fact that such birds always keep company with whalers so as to feed upon the remains of the giant mammal.

As I finished talking with another shipmate about this subject, an enormous albatross came sailing majestically through the air toward us. This was the largest bird I had ever seen, and little wonder, for no bird that flies has a wider wingspan. Soon after that, another arrived; and, although we were more than a thousand miles from any shore, we were scented out and surrounded by hosts of gonies, stinkards, haglets, gulls, and other sea birds. These creatures lost no time in beginning to feed on pieces of the whale's carcass with savage gluttony. After periods of feeding, these greedy birds could only fly away with great difficulty. No doubt that they would need to take days to digest their large meal!

Sharks, too, came to get their share of the prize whale. These savage man-eaters, however, did not content themselves with what was thrown away. They were bold enough to come before our faces and take bites out of the whale's body. Many of these sharks were over nine feet long, and when I saw them open their horrid jaws, armed with three rows of sharp glistening teeth, I could well understand how easily they could bite off the leg of a man if given the opportunity. Sometimes they would come right up on the whale's body with a wave, bite out great pieces of the flesh, and then roll off.

While I was looking over the side during the early part of that day, I saw a very large shark come lunging up in this way close to the first mate's legs. Mr. Owens took a swipe at it with his blubber-spade, but the man-eater rolled off in time to escape the blow. As I watched this scene, I wondered to myself if Mr. Owens had even managed to frighten the seemingly fearless aggressor. Surely, an experienced sailor like the first mate had to know how difficult it was to frighten, let alone kill, a large shark.

"Hand me an iron and line, Jim," said Mr. Owens, looking up at me. "I've got a score to settle with this here shark who is stealing our profits. He's been up in my direction twice now, nipping at my toes. Look sharp, lad, and hand down the harpoon. I will need two or three of ye to stand by and hold on to the other end of the line. There he comes, the big villain!"

Before I could manage to register a concern with the agitated first mate, I saw the shark move violently toward Mr. Owens, who promptly sent the harpoon right down its throat.

"Hold on hard now, me hearties," shouted the first mate.

"Aye, aye," we all replied, as we held on to the line. Within moments, we could feel our arms jerking wildly as the giant shark tried to free himself. We quickly positioned the line through a block and tackle at the fore yardarm and began to haul the man-eater on deck. The scene that followed was more than we bargained for in terms of danger, for there was no killing the beast. It threshed the deck with its tail and snapped so fiercely with its tremendous jaws that it was a wonder that none of us lost a leg or two in the struggle. At last its tail was cut off, the body cut open, and all the entrails taken out. Much to our amazement, however, this powerful brute continued to flap around the deck for some time, while his heart continued to contract for twenty minutes after he had been cut open.

I would not have believed that any shark could have been so powerful or tenacious unless I had seen it with my own eyes. The other shipmates, even those who had been on numerous voyages over the years, had to confess that they had seldom, if ever, seen a more amazing man-eater.

Mr. Owens claimed the skin of the shark for himself, as it could be sold to sailors after cleaning and drying, as sandpaper. Sailors often like to polish the things that they make out of whales' bones and teeth and are, therefore, willing to pay for sharkskin.

Shortly after the incident with the shark, our crew cut the last piece of blubber off of our whale. After this, Captain Flynn inspected the inside cavity of the whale, searching for a treasure known as ambergris. This special substance, worth hundreds of dollars a pound, was used to make expensive perfume. Few sailors ever found ambergris, for it was normally only located within the body cavity of a sick whale.

After the inspection, the order was given by the captain to cast off the useless remains of the whale. The unsecured carcass sank like a stone, much to the sorrow of the smaller birds which, having been driven away by their bigger comrades, had not fed as heartily as they had wished. But what was loss to the gulls was gain to the sharks, who could follow the carcass down into the deep and devour it at their leisure.

Even when the whale was gone, however, there was still plenty of danger. Its juices made the deck and cutting stage slippery. Sailors were in constant risk of slipping overboard to the sharks, or of slashing themselves on knives or sharp equipment. Apart from the slippery conditions, crewmen were at risk to be crushed by two-ton pieces of blubber. Nevertheless, there was still a certain amount of relief that took place in the minds of both captain and crew when the whale was finally butchered and his carcass released.

"Now, lads," cried the second mate, when the remains had vanished, "rouse up the fires; look alive, ye whale men!"

"Aye, aye, sir," was the ready reply, cheerfully given, as every man moved into his appointed duty.

And so, having cut in our whale, we then proceeded to try out the oil.

CHAPTER 8

Oil and Trouble

The life of a whale man on the high seas is often one of extremes. One minute he is floating on a calm sea trying to find something to occupy his mind, and the next minute he is in a life and death battle with a whale, or perhaps a shark.

The greatest evil, by far, in a whale man's life is when he has nothing to do. In such circumstances, days seem to stagnate into dreary nights where men have little else to think on but the pain of being separated from family and friends.

When the crew engaged in the smelly and tiresome task of "trying out" the oil, they seldom complained, for although it was not a particularly thrilling job, it was still recognized as being immensely preferable to inactivity. Whatever else may be said about the processing of whale oil, at least it kept the men's energies and minds well occupied.

Before we began to try out the oil, Captain Flynn called to the crew. "All hands aft to splice the main brace!"

The captain passed the traditional jug of grog out to the men and ordered that a meal be dished out. Although I passed over the grog, the meal was a welcome sight. This celebration turned out to be a brief and festive break, for the captain could not afford to lose the opportunity to complete the trying out of the oil while the seas were calm.

Our crew was soon divided into two watches, each taking a shift of six hours of hard labor through the day and night. Once the fires were lit and the trying out work begun, the captain tried to finish the work completely, without interruption.

The "try works" consisted of two, or sometimes three, huge

melting pots mounted upon brick fireplaces between the fore and main masts. Mr. Owens ordered some of the men to boil out the oil from the whale's head, or "case," while still others he sent to light the fires under the try pots. The fires were started with wood, but as the hours passed, the fire would be fed with the oily scraps of blubber that were readily available.

Most of the other men from our work crew were sent down to the blubber-room to help cut up the "blanket pieces," as the largest masses are called, while other men cut them up into smaller chunks called "horse pieces." Hour after hour, men stood near tall and sturdy blocks of wood, called "horses," and cut the chunks of blubber with mincing knives into uniform slices known as "Bible leaves." The chunks of blubber were slashed in an effort to help them melt more easily.

On a regular basis, the men at the try-pots would shout "Bible leaves! Bibles leaves!" to indicate that more of the processed chunks of blubber needed to be thrown into the melting pots by one of the mates. As the boiling oil rose in the pots, it was bailed into copper cooling tanks. Eventually, this oil was transferred into standard wooden barrels and stowed away in the hold of our ship.

As nighttime approached on the *Landsman,* the fires from the try-pots became redder and brighter by contrast. A strange light shone and glit-  tered on our bloody deck, as our crew forged ahead with its dirty work. For some strange reason, I could not help thinking, "What would my mother say if she could get a peep at me now?"

The time finally came for our watch to retire for six hours of welcome rest. As I slept, the new watch kept the fires burning and continued to process the remains of the giant creature.

When I awoke, I walked over to the windlass and sat down to enjoy a delicious breakfast consisting of beans and stale biscuits. While I was eating, one of my shipmates, Fred Hammer by name, sat down beside me. He was one of the younger members of the crew, at nineteen, and we seemed to get along well from the start. As I continued eating, he spoke.

"I fear we are going to have a breeze, Jim," he said, as a sharp puff of wind crossed the deck, driving the smoke leeward.

"I hope it won't be a storm, then," said I, "for it will oblige us to put out the fires. More than one sailor has been scalded in times past trying to work the try-pots in troubled seas."

"It's not just the scalding that I'm worried about, Jim," said Fred. "A far worse danger arises on board when a strong wind begins to spread the fires beneath the pots to other parts of the ship! Just last year, the schooner *J. Truman* caught fire in this very way and sank to the bottom with all hands."

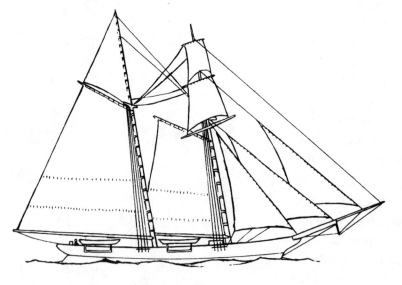

Topsail Schooner

I never found out how the fire got out of control on this ship, for at that moment the captain came on deck, and gave orders to furl the top gallant sails. Three or four of my shipmates were soon climbing upward on the rigging like monkeys; and, in a few minutes, the sails were lashed to the yards.

The wind soon began to blow steadily from the nor' west, but not hard enough to stop our try-works for more than an hour. After that, the wind blew stiff enough to raise a heavy sea, and we were compelled to slack the fires. Much to Captain Flynn's delight, however, this was all the harm this brief tempest caused. It never did develop into a dangerous gale.

As the captain and the first mate walked the quarterdeck together, I heard the former say to the latter, "I think we had as well take in the reefs in the topsails. All hereabouts the fishing-ground is good, we don't need to carry on."

The order was given to reduce sail, and the men lay out on the topsail yards. I noticed that my friend, Fred Hammer, was the first man to spring up the shroud lines and lay out on the main topsail yard. It was so dark on account of the storm clouds that I could scarcely see the masts. While I was gazing up, I thought I observed a dark object drop from the yard. At the same moment, there was a loud shriek, followed by a noise in the sea. In a matter of seconds, my fears were confirmed as I heard someone cry, "Man overboard!" and instantly the whole ship was in an uproar.

Only those sailors who have heard that cry can understand the dreadful feelings that are raised in the human breast by it. My heart, at first, seemed to leap into my throat and almost choke me. Then a terrible fear, which I cannot describe, shot through me, when I thought that it might be my comrade Fred Hammer. But those thoughts and feelings passed like lightning—in a far shorter time than it takes to write them down. The cry of the falling sailor was still ringing in my ears when the captain roared:

"Down with your helm! Stand by to lower away the boats!"

At the same moment, he seized a light hencoop and tossed it overboard, and the first mate did the same with an oar in the twinkling of an eye. Almost without knowing what I did or why I did it, I grabbed a great pile of oak scraps that were lying on the deck saturated with oil and placed them in a large shovel nearby. I thrust the shovel into the edge of the fire under the try-works, and hurled them blazing into the sea.

The ship's head was thrown into the wind and we were brought to as quickly as possible. A gleam of hope arose within me on observing that the mass I had thrown overboard still continued to burn. But when I saw how quickly the little fires went astern, not withstanding our vigorous efforts to stop the ship, my heart began to sink. A few moments later, the situation turned more desperate after the little lights suddenly disappeared. Despair was quickly setting in, as I prepared myself for the fact that my friend may well be lost forever.

At that moment, strange to say, thoughts of my mother came into my mind. I remembered her words, "Call upon the Lord, my dear boy, when you are in trouble." Although I had permitted the worldly atmosphere of a whaling vessel to significantly compromise my prayer life and Christian testimony, I did earnestly pray, then and there, that my messmate might be saved. I cannot say that my prayer of desperation was very impressive to God; still, the mere act of crying in my distress to the Almighty afforded me some real relief. It is often at times such as this that the Lord chooses to remind us of how helpless we really are as creatures, and how utterly dependent we are on Him for life, safety, and success.

The captain ordered each man to his station in the long boats and yelled, "Lower away!"

It was with a good deal of energy that I threw myself into the first boat that was lowered, and pulled on the oars as if my life depended on it.

The second mate, who was the headsman of our boat, had

fastened a lantern to the end of an oar and set it up in the bow. By its faint light we could see but a short distance off.

"Do you think we have any chance of finding him, sir?" I asked.

A shake of the head was his only reply, until a strange noise was heard. "Hold on, lads; did anyone hear a cry?"

No one answered. We all ceased pulling and listened intently. The noise of the whistling wind and waves were all that could be heard.

"What's that floating on the water?" said one of the men suddenly.

"Where away?" cried the second mate.

"Right off the lee-bow—there, don't you see it?" questioned the crewman.

At that moment a faint cry came floating over the black water, and died away in the breeze. The simple word "Hurrah!" burst from our throats with all the power of our lungs, and we bent to our oars till we well nigh tore the rowlocks out of the boat.

"Hold hard! Stern all!" roared the mate, as we went flying down to leeward and almost ran over the hencoop, to which a human form was seen to be clinging with the determination of a drowning man. In our zeal we managed to shoot past our shipmate, and I became concerned that we would lose him again. The fear of losing Fred caused me to panic as I leaped up and sprang into the sea.

Thanks be to God, however, that Ben Lodins had the presence of mind to seize me by my jacket just as I reached the water, so as to prevent me from leaving the side of the boat. Two of my shipmates pulled me aboard a short time later, as we maneuvered in the direction of my friend. In a few moments more, after I received a stern tongue lashing from the second mate for jumping ship, we reached the hencoop and rescued Fred Hammer.

He was half dead with cold and exhaustion, poor fellow, but by the time we reached the *Landsman* he was beginning to recover strength. His first words were to thank God for His deliverance. Then he added:

"And thanks to the man that flung that light overboard. I could have gone down but for the fact that it showed me where the hencoop was."

I cannot describe the feeling of joy that filled my heart when he finished his comments. "Aye, who was it that threw that fire overboard?" inquired one of the men.

"Don't know," replied another, "I think it may have been the captain."

"You'll find out when we get aboard," insisted the second mate. "Pull away, lads."

Within five minutes, we were all back on board, safe and sound. The rescued sailor was given a fresh set of dry clothes and wrapped up in a heavy wool blanket. A hot brick was placed near his feet, for good measure, and a mug of hot tea was also placed within his shivering hands.

As several of the crew sat staring at Fred Hammer, the captain bellowed, "All right ye blooming bunch of nannies, stop your staring now. In case you hadn't noticed, we still have work to do on this here ship. Mr. Owens, order the fire stoked and the men to resume their duties. The wind has slackened, and we must finish with our fish by morning so we can sail out of these waters."

"Aye, aye, Captain Flynn," came the reply.

CHAPTER 9

Big Tom the Fighting Bull

When the last of the whale oil was stored safely in the hold, we set sail in a southeasterly direction for the whaling grounds just off the cape of South Africa.

Weeks passed as we slowly made our way to the Crozettes hunting area, picking up an occasional right whale or overzealous shark on the way. We had already been at sea for several months, stopping only for fresh water at remote islands on our outward-bound track. Much to the delight of Captain Argus Flynn, who lately seemed to be in an agitated state of mind, we reached the South Sea hunting grounds off Cape Town. The captain had made a point of steering our whaler into seas that were well known for harboring giant sperm whales, some as long as seventy feet. He was tired of catching "suckers" or "calfs" as he called them and pledged a gold coin to the first man who sighted a big "school-master," or bull sperm whale.

One day, I turned to the first mate, Mr. Owens, and asked, "What's been eating the captain?"

After several seconds of contemplation, the tall and seasoned officer simply shrugged his shoulders and said, "He wants to catch the biggest sperm whale in this here sea. If you must know, I reckon he's after Big Tom himself."

"If ye don't mind me asking, sir," I continued, "who is this creature named Big Tom?"

"Why only the fiercest bull in all the four oceans, my young shipmate. He is marked by virtue of the five lances that protrude from his lumpy back, like so many peacock feathers. It was last fall that he was spotted in these waters, and I only hope that if we meet up with him that we fare better than the last hunting party."

"Why would that be, Mr. Owens?" I asked.

"The last time whaling men went after this monster, he managed to stove three boats and kill nearly a dozen men. The legend of Tom grows each year; some say that he has sunk whalers and killed over a hundred men. Others believe that he is a ghost and can't be captured or killed."

"Ye are not trying to frighten me with one of those wild stories about monster whales are you, sir?"

"I say what I say," asserted the first mate, sharply, as he slowly walked away.

Moments later, as I approached a group of shipmates who had just finished their watch, one of them shouted, "Chanteyman, give us a song!" "How about *Carlingford*?" added another mate.

As the men gathered around me, amidst the swaying of the sails, I lifted my voice and sang the opening verse:

"When I was young and in my prime and could wander wild and free, there was always the longing in my mind to follow the call of the sea."

The assembled shipmates then provided the chorus to this old favorite by singing:

"Well I sing farewell to Carlingford, and farewell to Green Ore, and I think of you most day and night, until I return once more, until I return once more."

I then continued, "On all of the stormy seven seas, I have sailed before the mast, and on every voyage I ever made, I swore it would be my last."

After another chorus, I ended by singing, "Well a landsman's life is all his own, he can go where he can stay, but when the sea gets in your blood, when she calls you must obey. Well I sing farewell to

Carlingford and farewell to Green Ore, and I think of you most day and night, until I return once more, until I return once more."

As the noise of the song quickly floated away from the assembly, an even more delightful voice could be heard in the distance crying, "Supper, laddies!" The thoughts of the men soon turned to their stomachs as they prepared to feast on bread, soup, and a special ration of plum pudding.

A predictable hush fell over the men as they began to concentrate on their eating. I sat down next to my friend, Ben Lodins, who was talking with the second mate about the difference between the right whale and the sperm whale.

I listened intently as the second mate stated, "Although the right and sperm whales are both found in the South Seas, the sperm whale never ventures into the North Seas. Both creatures grow to an enormous size, but they look quite different from each other, especially in the shapes of their heads."

As the second mate paused, I asked, "Sir, can ye tell me about the look of a sperm whale? I've only seen the creature in pictures."

"Oh, yes," responded the junior officer. "The sperm whale's huge blunt head is about one third the size of its entire body. It looks somewhat like a big log with the end sawn square off. The lower jaw of this creature has large white teeth, yet there are no teeth in the upper jaw. Unlike the right whale, the sperm whale has only one blowhole, and that a little one, much farther forward on its head. Whale men can often spot a sperm whale at a great distance by noting the manner in which it spouts close to the front of its blunt head."

Ben Lodins, who was quite well acquainted with whales, went on to describe the habits and might of the sperm whale by adding:

"The sperm whale feeds differently than the right whale. It seizes its prey with its powerful jaws and teeth, and swallows its meal whole. It lives, to a great extent, on large cuttlefish. Some of these whales have been seen to vomit up lumps of these cuttlefish as long as a whaleboat. This giant is more aggressive, too, than the right whale, which often takes to flight when struck. Sperm whales are noted for their aggressiveness after being wounded, and will sometimes turn on their foes and smash their boat with a blow of its blunt head or tail. Wise old sperm whales, called 'bulls,' which have become clever through experience, give sailors the greatest trouble.

"It's not often that the sperm whale actually attacks a ship; but there are a few cases of this kind which cannot be doubted. The famous case involving the whaler *Essex* is widely known, and while it shows the power of a sperm whale, it also reveals what risk sailors take when they go after fighting bulls. Permit me to recount this amazing, true story.

"In the year of our Lord, 1819, the American whale ship *Essex* sailed from Nantucket for the Pacific Ocean. She was under the command of Captain Pollard. Late in the autumn of the same year, when in latitude 40 degrees of the South Seas, a 'school' of sperm whales was discovered. Three boats were immediately lowered and sent in pursuit. The first mate's boat was struck by one of the bulls during a chase, and it became necessary for this vessel to return to the *Essex* for repairs.

"While the crewmen were busy taking care of their damaged boat, an enormous whale suddenly rose quite close to the ship. He was going at nearly the same speed as the *Essex*, about three knots. The men on board the ship could easily see that this giant sperm whale was no less than eighty-five feet in length. All at once the monster ran against the ship, causing her to tremble like a leaf. The whale immediately dove and passed under the ship, grazing the keel with its back. This act evidently injured the giant bull, for he suddenly rose to the surface about fifty yards off and proceeded to lash the sea with his tail as if in great agony.

"In a short time, however, the beast seemed to recover and swam off in a windward direction. Meanwhile, the men on board the *Essex* discovered that the blow had done so much damage to the ship that she had begun to fill and settle down at the bows. As quickly as possible, the crewmembers rigged a pump together so they could keep the ship afloat. While the men worked frantically to save the ship, one of the sailors cried out:

" 'God have mercy! He comes again!'

"This was all too true. The whale had turned and was now bearing down on them at full speed, leaving a white track of foam behind him. Rushing headlong at the wounded ship like a battering ram, the creature hit her fair on the weather bow and stove it in. Soon after, the mighty sperm whale dove into the deep and disappeared.

"The horrified men took to their long boats at once, and in ten minutes the *Essex* went down beneath the waves. The condition of the men thus left in three open boats far out upon the sea, without provisions or shelter, was terrible indeed.

"Some of the sailors perished during the long voyage to find land, and the rest, after suffering the severest hardships, reached a small island called Ducies on the twentieth of December. It was little more than a sand bank, which supplied them only with water and seafowl. Under the circumstances, however, even this was a mercy from God, for many of their men were slowly dying from dehydration.

"Three of the crew members resolved to remain on this tiny island, for dreary and uninhabited though it was, they preferred to take their chances of being picked up by a passing ship rather than run the risks of crossing the wide ocean in open boats with little fresh water. After a sorrowful farewell, the men who declined to stay on the remote island slowly rowed away.

"It was on the twenty-seventh of December when the three boats left the sandbank with the remainder of the men, and began a new voyage of two thousand miles toward the island of Juan Fernandez. The mate's boat was picked up about three months later by the ship *Indian* of London. It only had three living souls. Around the same time, the captain's boat was discovered by the *Dauphin* of Nantucket, with only two living men. These pathetic beings had only managed to stay alive by feeding on the remains of their dead comrades. The third boat must have been lost, for it was never recovered.

"Out of a crew of twenty men, only five survived to tell their amazing story, for the three men who were determined to stay on the remote island were never heard from again."

"Tell me, Ben," said I. "Why were the men on the island never found?"

"Seems as though the tiny island was so far out of the usual path of ships that no vessel came close enough to discover them."

As my shipmate Ben Lodins prepared to continue his talk, a

loud cry could be heard coming from the crow's nest.

"There she blows! Big whales off the starboard bow!"

This unexpected alarm made us all spring to our feet in an awkward fashion. As the *Landsman* maneuvered into position for the hunt, the deck hands strained their necks to be the first one to sight a big bull whale. Every crew member longed to get the gold coin that was pledged by Argus Flynn.

"There she breaches! There she blows!" cried the lookout, once again.

The captain soon appeared on deck and shouted, "Where away?"

"Sperm whales, about two miles off the lee beam, sir."

Without as much as a word from the captain, every man moved into his proper position or station. After several months out at sea, our crew had become so accustomed to the routine that we acted together like a piece of machinery.

"Sing out when the ship heads for her," barked Captain Flynn as he moved to the masthead.

"Aye, aye, sir."

"Keep her away," ordered the captain to the helmsman. "Mr. Owens, hand me the spy-glass."

"Steady," came the cry from the masthead.

"Steady it is," answered the man at the helm.

While we were all looking eagerly ahead, we heard a thundering snort behind us, followed by a heavy splash. Turning around, we saw the flukes of an enormous whale sweeping through the air not more than six hundred yards astern of us.

"Down your helm!" roared the captain. "Haul up the mainsail and square the yards. Call all hands."

"All hands, ahoy!" ordered the second mate, with a voice that thundered. In a flash, all hands were on deck and ready for action.

"Hoist and swing the boats," uttered the anxious captain.

"Lower away."

Down went the boats into the water, almost before you could wink. We pulled away from the *Landsman* just as the whale rose the second time, about half a mile away to leeward.

Thanks to the instruction of Ben Lodins and the second mate, I had no trouble in identifying our target as a bull sperm whale. Everyone on board our whaleboat felt certain that it was the largest whale we had yet seen, so we pulled after it with right good will.

I occupied my usual place in the captain's boat, next to the bow-oar. Argus Flynn himself steered, and, as our crew was a picked one, we soon left the other two boats behind us.

Presently a small whale rose close beside us, and, sending a shower of mist over the boat, went down into a pool of foam. Before long, another whale rose gently on the opposite side of the boat, and then another off our starboard bow. Much to our delight, we found ourselves in the middle of a shoal of whales, which proceeded to leap and spout all around without any awareness of our violent intentions.

A few minutes later, however, the patience of our leader was rewarded as the large bull whale that we noted prior to leaving the *Landsman* came once again to the surface. By the wild and active manner in which this giant breached, we knew that we were in for a challenging hunt. After blowing on the surface once or twice, about a quarter of a mile off, he peaked his flukes and pitched down head first.

"Now then, lads, he's down for one last long dive," said the captain. "Spring your oars like men, and we will get that fish for certain when he breaches. Pull, ye sheep heads. This beast is not Big Tom, but he is a fine prize bull."

The captain was mistaken, however, for this prize whale had only gone down deep in order to come up and spring out of the water with reckless abandon. While Argus Flynn and crew gazed at the spectacle before them, several of the men gave a shout of wonder and alarm. Little wonder why, for this huge whale had managed to leap clear out of the water not a hundred yards from the boat.

The awkward creature came down on his side with a thundering crash that might well have been heard six miles off. As his big white belly and massive gray head plunged beneath the sea, a mountain of spray burst from the spot where he fell, and in another moment he was gone.

"I wonder still, Captain, if that bull is not Big Tom," shouted the harpooner.

"I doubt it," responded Captain Flynn, "but it is pretty clear that he's an old sperm bull. Give way, lads, we must capture that whale whatever it should cost us."

We did not need a second bidding, for the size of the whale was so impressive that we felt more excited than we had yet been during the voyage. Without hesitation, we bent our oars till we almost pulled the boat out of the water. As we moved along the surface of the water, I noted with some interest that we were chasing this whale all by ourselves. The other boats had become separated in the confusion and were busy chasing smaller whales.

"There she blows," said our leader in a low voice, as the brute came up a short distance astern of us.

We had overshot our mark, so, turning about, we made for the whale, which was clinging near the surface. The giant slowly turned to windward and spouted from his big square head as we approached.

Thanks, in part, to the skillful steering of our captain, we finally got within a few feet of the monster. At this point, the captain suddenly ordered the harpooner to stand up.

The anxious harpooner jumped up in an instant with his weapon, and skillfully buried a harpoon deep in the blubber.

"Stern all!" was the next word, as we backed off with all our might. This maneuver was just in time, for, in his agony, the whale tossed his tail right over our heads. The flukes of this giant were so big that they could have completely covered our boat. Thanks be to God, however, the sperm bull we harpooned decided to bring down his huge flukes flat on the sea with a loud clap that made our ears tingle.

For a brief moment, I thought that we were going to be crushed to death, but we soon found ourselves out of immediate danger. Needless to say, we were soaked to the skin by the spray sent upon us by the frantic whale. All we could manage to do at this point was to lie on our oars and watch the wounded monster lash the ocean into foam. The water all around us soon became white, like milk, while the foam near the whale turned red with blood.

Suddenly, the sperm whale ceased his thrashing, and, before we could row over and lance him, plunged deep into the sea. This unexpected maneuver took our line out at such a rate that our boat spun completely around. Sparks of fire soon flew from the logger head from the chafing of the rope.

"Hold on!" cried the captain, who was trying to remain calm. The next moment, we were tearing over the sea at a fearful rate, while the waves threatened to swamp us. I instinctively began to pray to the Almighty, as our predicament became more and more life threatening. As I glanced around the boat, I was somewhat comforted to see that several other men were also conversing with their Maker and pleading for mercy. Never before had I experienced so much danger.

While we were tearing over the water, we noticed other whales coming up every now and then near our vessel. At one point, we passed close enough to the first mate's boat to see that he was also tied to a whale, and unable, therefore, to render us any help.

Our line finally began to slacken, so we hauled it in hand over hand and coiled it away in the tub at the stern of the boat. During this momentary pause in the action, Captain Flynn took his place in the bow and prepared to utilize his lance. The whale soon surfaced and we promptly rowed toward him. This time, however, the clever giant did not run away but turned around and made straight for our little boat.

I was now so certain that destruction was at hand that I did not bother either to panic or pray, for the great blunt forehead of the sperm bull was coming down on us like a steamboat. As it turned out, my assumption was in error, for our leader reached out and savagely pricked the head of the whale, and he turned away in a different direction to avoid the pain.

We continued to pursue the wise old bull, seeking for the right moment to finish him off. At last he turned a little to one side, and the captain plunged the lance deep into his vitals.

"Ha! That's touched his life," cried Ben Lodins as blood flew up from the creature's blowhole. This was evidence that the mighty giant had been mortally wounded. But he was not yet conquered. After receiving the cruel stab with the lance, he pitched down and once more began to fly out over the sea. We tried to hold fast, but the bull had gone down too deeply and we had to slack off our line to prevent being pulled under the waves.

As the line flew out, one of the coils in the tub became tangled.

"Look out, lads!" yelled Ben, as he tried to clear the line. The captain, in trying to do the same thing, slipped and fell. Seeing this, I sprang up, and, grasping the coil as it flew past, tried to clear it. Before I could think, however, a section of rope whipped around my left wrist. I felt a wrench as if my arm would be torn out of the socket, and in a moment I was overboard.

A moment later, I found myself going down with great speed into the depths of the sea. Strange to say, I did not lose my presence of mind. I was fully aware of what was happening as the rushing water went whizzing past my eyes. A dreadful pressure began to build up in my ears as the creature took me down into the depths. Yet, even in that difficult moment, thoughts of eternity, of my sins, and of meeting the Lord flashed into my mind. Would I ever live to see another sunrise?

Before I could contemplate my circumstance further, I felt myself slowly rising toward the surface. It is impossible for me to say exactly how I became freed from the rope, but I suppose the turn of the line must have slacked off somehow. As hope renewed itself within me, I began to buffet the water in an effort to reach the surface. Just when I was about to lose consciousness, my head finally broke the surface of the water.

After I came into the land of the living once again and looked about me, I saw the boat not more than fifty yards off. Being a good swimmer, I struck out for it, although I felt terribly exhausted. A few minutes later, my shipmates saw me, and, with a cheer, put out the oars and began to row toward me. I noted that the line was slack, and that they were hauling it in—a sign that the whale had ceased running. Before they had pulled half-a-dozen strokes, however, I watched in horror as the monstrous head of the whale shot up like a great rock out of the deep not five feet away from the boat.

I heard the captain cry, "Stern all!" But it was too late, for the whole weight of the monster's body fell upon the tiny vessel. A terrible crashing sound could be heard, mingled with the cries of the men.

For a few moments the wounded giant continued to lash the sea in his fury, as the fragments of the fractured boat floated all about him. I was under the assumption that every man, of course, had been killed. As the spray began to lessen, however, one after another of my shipmate's heads appeared in the midst of the blood and foam. These survivors soon began to swim toward any object that was floating in the water.

Providentially, the unpredictable whale had overshot his target by a few feet; else every man would surely have perished. It was not long before I was able to join my comrades in the search for something upon which to float. My strength was nearly gone as I seized upon an oar that had come within my reach.

Just then I heard a cheer, and the next time I rose on the swell,

I looked round and saw the first mate's boat headed for the scene of action. After what seemed like a long time, I was finally hauled out of the ocean by men from the third boat. By God's grace, no sailors were killed in the hunt, although one of them had a leg broken, and another an arm twisted out of joint.

After the captain was fished out of the cold waters, he ordered the remaining boats to secure the wounded whale who was about ready to breathe his last.

"Fast again, hurrah!" shouted the mate as he grabbed his lance and ordered his men to attack. He gave the monster two deep stabs, and then retreated while the animal began to move into its death roll.

I could not look upon the dying struggles of this majestic giant without feelings of regret and reproach for helping to destroy it. I felt almost as if I were a murderer, and that the Creator would call me to account for taking part in the destruction of one of His grandest living creatures. But the thought quickly left my mind as the whale became more violent and finished his death flurry. We gazed at this scene in deep silence and with hearts torn between remorse and jubilation.

All at once, the struggler ceased. The great carcass rolled over belly up in death. The calm that followed was quite amazing, after all the minutes spent in noisy battle. The silence, however, was suddenly broken by three hearty cheers, which were followed by an urgent effort to fasten a towrope to our prize. The process of towing the sperm whale to the *Landsman* required the rest of the afternoon, for we had no fewer than eight miles to pull.

As our crowded boat came closer to the *Landsman,* the first mate began to stare into the distance with a strange expression of fear and wonder.

"Mr. Owens," I called. "Have ye seen a ghost, sir?"

Without any comment at all, the first mate simply pointed off the starboard bow to a huge gray creature with five lances protruding out of its back.

As the crusty old bull swam angrily by, no one could manage to speak. In this instance, words were quite unnecessary, for it was evident to all that we were staring at none other than Big Tom himself.

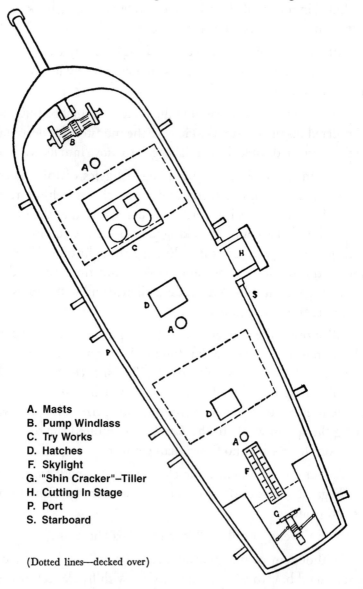

A. Masts
B. Pump Windlass
C. Try Works
D. Hatches
F. Skylight
G. "Shin Cracker"–Tiller
H. Cutting In Stage
P. Port
S. Starboard

(Dotted lines—decked over)

Deck layout of typical whaling vessel

CHAPTER 10

Death on the High Seas

Under normal conditions, the whale that we had just taken would have been enough to gratify the sternest captain. It was clearly the largest catch of that season, and produced over ninety barrels of fine oil. Nevertheless, Captain Flynn was still agitated about losing his chance to capture Big Tom. In fact, it might be more proper to state that our captain was fast becoming obsessed with bringing in this legendary bull.

Up to this time our voyage had gone prosperously. We had caught so many whales that nearly half our quota was already complete. By Mr. Owens's estimates, he reckoned that we might well be able to return home to old New Bedford sooner than originally expected.

Of course, during all this time we had met with some disappointments, for I am not describing everything that happened on our voyage. Time permits me to recount for you only the major adventures that we experienced as whale men.

By the evening of the second day after we spotted Big Tom, we were already finishing up the cutting and trying out of our third whale. Everyone, with the exception of the captain, was in good spirits and looking forward to a great season of hunting. One of our crew was particularly happy at this time for he discovered a chunk of the valuable substance called ambergris as he helped to process one of our recent catches. During a lull in our work, I sat listening to the captain as he called all hands to the main deck.

"Mr. Owens," said the captain. "Fetch the gold piece in my quarters. It is time to reward the lookout who spotted that fine bull sperm two days hence."

A minute or two later, the first mate strolled across the deck and handed the shiny gold coin to the captain. "Step forward, mate, and claim your reward," shouted the captain as he struggled to rouse himself out of his melancholy state.

Moments later, the keen-eyed lookout stepped forward and received his impressive reward.

"Now," began Captain Flynn, "I pledge two gold coins to the man who finds me Big Tom. Will ye drink with me, boys? Will ye drink to the death of Big Tom? Mr. Owens," continued the captain, who by now was in a fit of passion, "break out the full measure of grog!"

Shouts of approval quickly rang in the air, as the men prepared to partake of strong drink. For my part, I hardly saw the point in celebrating in this fashion, for strong drink never held any attraction for me. As I looked over in the direction of my friend, Fred Hammer, it was evident that he was also disturbed by the whole scene.

"We must pull together, lads, as one man in our quest to kill old Tom," continued the captain. "All ye that are true whale men will not fail to drink from this jug. Come heaven or hell, men, we must not leave these waters until Tom spouts black blood and rolls over dead!"

I was not sure who it was that addressed us from the main deck, for it was surely not the same Argus Flynn that sailed with us out of New Bedford. If I did not know better, I would certainly have concluded at that moment that Captain Flynn had gone mad. His very countenance and spirit was the picture of folly and darkness. The more I contemplated the whole attitude of our formerly levelheaded leader, the more my soul withdrew in fear.

As the jug of grog was passed to me, I was unable to summon the courage to pass it by as I had routinely done in the past. I, therefore, pretended to drink from the jug, to pacify the demands of Captain Flynn, and quickly handed it off to my friend Fred Hammer. As the so-called celebration of unity continued, all eyes were fixed on my friend, as he stood motionless with the jug at his side.

"Drink deep and quickly, man!" shouted the captain in an agitated voice.

"Sir," responded my shipmate Fred, "I have sworn an oath since my youth not to touch strong drink."

"Oh," said Argus Flynn, "are ye a Quaker boy, then?" hoping to humiliate the principled young sailor.

"No sir," stated Fred. "But what I am is a man seeking to keep his word. When a man gives a pledge to his Maker, he should keep it. I will not judge you, Captain, in regard to meat and drink. All I ask is to be left alone to decide whether or not to partake of strong drink."

"Enough of this nonsense and babbling," asserted the captain rudely. "If I want to hear a sermon, boy, I will pay a visit to the Seaman's Bethel. Go on then, pass the jug to the real whale man standing next to ye."

I, for one, was sickened by the whole exchange between Argus Flynn and my friend Fred. Perhaps what was more disheartening about the experience, however, was the discovery of how little moral courage I possessed within my soul. After the little celebration was over and we all returned to our duties, I tried to be particularly kind to my shipmate Fred, for he was clearly downcast.

As I struggled to shake off the events of that evening, I was glad to spend some time alone in the bow of the *Landsman*. After much prayer and contemplation, I resolved to make a greater effort to live out my faith with the same courage as Fred Hammer. In many respects, the hours that I spent staring at the waves and communing with the Lord were of immense spiritual benefit to me. As later events would reveal, God was strengthening me for even greater trials that He was about to send my way.

The next morning, after a hearty breakfast of oatmeal and biscuits, I walked over to the windlass and sat down on a large barrel located nearby. As I sat whistling a favorite tune, I watched five men who were in my vicinity. Some of the men were busy sharpening harpoons and cutting knives, while others were making all kinds of toys or gifts out of their whale's bones.

After several minutes, I became somewhat restless and began to stroll the deck in search of something to do. As I passed by a group of my shipmates, I heard one of them describing in mournful terms how the whale that he recently harpooned and killed sank to the bottom before it could be towed to the *Landsman*. Upon hearing this tale, I simply smiled to myself, for such disappointments were the common lot of a whale man.

One week passed, rather uneventfully, as our quest for the legendary whale continued. As might be expected, the talk among the men ranged from the change in the captain's attitude to that of who would win the coveted gold coins for spotting Big Tom. This particular day, being Sunday, was given over to rest or to light duty so the atmosphere on board was quite mellow.

Fred Hammer and a few other men joined me early in the forenoon for a time of Bible reading and worship. As prayers were lifted up by each of the men in attendance, it was evident that each of us was concerned for the spiritual estate of Argus Flynn. Although the captain was commonly regarded as a decent man, he was not known to be a Christian or even a Sabbath keeper.

The longer we prayed and talked together after services, the more we became convinced of the goodness of God in placing us on a whaler that seldom required hard labor on the Sabbath. It should be known that whaling men, as a rule, do not concern themselves with spiritual things. Most whaling men don't let the Lord's Day interfere with their selfish ambitions. Besides which, it is the rule of the sea that the captain's orders must be obeyed, even if his orders may come on Sunday.

Thankfully, no whales of any size were spotted on that Lord's

Day, so the issue of going after whales on Sunday soon passed from our minds.

The new week opened on a hopeful note, as our crew spotted and killed two right whales and one sperm whale. Although the sperm whale was a modest sized creature, he was not to be compared to the two right whales, which fetched us almost sixty barrels each. For the first time in days, I actually saw Captain Flynn laugh with one of his officers. I was hopeful that this was an indication that he was beginning to recover from his melancholy state.

The remainder of this week was quiet as the crew busied itself with storing barrels in the hold and cleaning up the ship. During this same period, Captain Flynn sailed the *Landsman* over to the nearby port city of Cape Town, in order to secure needed provisions and fresh water. Only the anxiousness of our captain prevented us from going ashore at this place.

Before we knew it, it was the Lord's Day once again. After services, several men stood around telling stories of high sea adventure, mixed with a good dose of humor and malarkey. There are few things in life that a sailor loves more than a good story or yarn, and soon the *Landsman's* deck was filled with laughter.

All of a sudden, the man at the mast's head sang out that a large sperm whale was spouting away two points off the port bow. This call came as a particular surprise, for it had been many months since our crew had spotted any large whale on a Sunday.

As usual, Captain Flynn rushed up to the main deck and yelled, "Is it Big Tom?"

"Can't say for sure, Captain," came the reply. "All I know is that it looks like a big sperm bull."

Without hesitation, Captain Flynn gave the order to ready the boats for lowering. As the thought never entered my mind to disobey a direct order, I went like the rest to my usual station.

To the surprise of everyone, however, Fred Hammer, instead

of going to his post, went up to the captain with a red face and, touching his cap, said: "Please, sir, it is the Sabbath day. I–I–would rather not go after the whales today, sir."

Those of us who were within earshot opened our eyes wide in amazement, and some of the crew laughed out loud. The captain, however, looked sternly around and ordered silence.

Trying in vain to control his anger, Argus Flynn shouted, "And, pray, may I ask you why you are choosing to disobey a direct order?"

"Because, sir, God's Word forbids working at our ordinary calling on His day," responded Fred respectfully.

I knew poor Fred's gentle spirit well, and I could see from the expression on his face and the heaving of his chest how deeply he felt the sneers of his shipmates and the contempt of his captain.

"Did you not know when you shipped with me that you might need to work on Sunday as well as on any other day?" demanded the captain.

"Yes, sir, I did; but I did not think about the claims of God upon my life as seriously as I now do. My life has been saved from a watery grave, as you know, but a short time ago, and God has opened my eyes to see my duty to obey His orders first and last."

Argus Flynn was a bit softened by this simple response, but the calming effect of my friend's speech did not last long; for one of the sailors began to laugh once again and rekindled the captain's anger.

"Go, sir," he said sternly. "Go to your duty. There will be time enough for you to preach when you are appointed chaplain to this ship. Disobey my orders, if you dare!"

Young Hammer hung his head, and turning slowly away, went to his usual station. By this time, every man on board was in his proper place.

"There she blows! There she breeches!" sung the lookout. "It's Big Tom for sure, Captain."

"Lower away!" roared the captain.

The boats were in the water and the men in position in one minute's time, but Fred hesitated. He well understood the stern punishment that awaited mutineers, but he also thought of the eternal punishment that willful sinners had to endure in the fires of hell.

The God-fearing sailor summoned the courage to stand on his convictions, regardless of the earthly cost and, turning around boldly, stated: "Sir, I cannot go—"

Before he could say another word, however, Argus Flynn rushed at Fred, seized him by the neck and hurled him over the side into the waiting long boat. In a matter of a few moments, the boat was away from the *Landsman's* side and on its way to do battle with a mighty sperm whale.

Some of the men in Fred's boat made an attempt to laugh at him, but it was quite plain that most of them regarded their young shipmate with greater respect than ever. As for me, I felt my heart drawn out to him, as I prayed that I might gain the courage to side with him openly in the future. The excitement of the battle that lay immediately before us, however, soon turned our thoughts away from what had just passed.

As we began to pull our way across the ocean, every man attempted to brace himself for a long and memorable fight. The whale that we were after was a very large and clever one, for it took almost two hours of hard pulling to get near enough to throw a harpoon in him. After we finally fixed a harpoon in the creature's side, he jumped clean out of the water and rushed forward at tremendous speed. Then there was the usual battle and treacherous sleigh ride across the top of the ocean. As we all anticipated, the battle was fierce and long; so long, in fact, that we often wondered if we would have to return to the *Landsman* empty-handed.

It is astonishing to see the difference between the fighting capacities of whales. One creature will give you no trouble at all, even if it is very large. Another will take you six hours to try to subdue, and even then may still get away. In the case of Big Tom, it clearly was of the type that will fight you tooth and nail.

As we continued our quest to capture Tom, it made two separate runs at our boat, but the mate in command cleverly pricked it off with a lance. At last we gave it a severe wound, and immediately it dove.

"That blow was into his life," remarked Mr. Owens, as we sat waiting for him to come up again. The captain's boat was, at that time, only twenty yards off our port side.

As it turned out, we did not have to wait long for the bull to surface. The sudden slackening off of all the lines showed that the

whale was coming up. All at once, I saw a dark object rising directly under the captain's boat. Before I could make out what it was, almost before I could think, the boat flew up into the air, as if a powder magazine had exploded beneath it. The whale had come up and hit it with his head right on the keel, so that it was knocked into pieces. Immediately, the air filled with the cries of desperate men and with a strange assortment of oars, lances, and rope.

Amidst this confusion and chaos, few of us bothered to notice that the mighty foe named Big Tom was, at last, going into his flurry. Our first priority was to pick up our wounded comrades. They all came to the surface quickly enough, but while some made for the boats vigorously, others swam slowly and with pain. Clearly, many of the men were hurt, while one or two lay floating on the surface as if they were dead.

Most of the men had escaped with only a few cuts and bruises, but one poor sailor had his leg broken, and another his head badly damaged. The worst case, however, was that of poor Fred Hammer. He had a broken leg, and a severe wound in his side from a harpoon, which had buried itself into his flesh over the barbs. It was only with great difficulty that we could remove the harpoon from his side. We laid him in the stern of the boat and attempted to keep him as still as possible. As our wounded shipmate lay bleeding, he tried to speak to us in a faint voice. His first words were: "I'm dying, messmates."

"Don't say that, Fred," said I, while my heart sank within me. "Cheer up, my friend, you'll live to see brighter days and big whales yet. Try to take a swallow of fresh water from this canteen. It will do you good."

He shook his head gently, being too weak to reply.

We had killed a big whale that day, and every one of us knew that when he was "tried in" we would be able to begin our journey homeward. But there was no cheer given when the monster turned over on his side, for our hearts were very heavy. The pull to the ship that evening was quiet and dreary, not unlike that of a funeral procession.

The next day, Fred was worse, and we all saw that his words would come true— he was dying. I never saw a man so downcast in all my life as our captain was when he realized that all hope of recovery was gone. He was truly a broken man. He often walked about the deck, muttering to himself, as if he were deranged. On two occasions, I overheard him in his cabin groaning, and loudly stating that he "had been the death of the lad, both body and soul."

I was permitted to nurse my poor messmate, and I spent much of my time in reading the Bible to him, at his own request. Many a time did the captain come down to see him to implore his forgiveness. Although Fred clearly granted forgiveness to him, he would not utter another word. The captain assumed this was due to weakness, but I felt sure there must be some other reason.

One day, before Fred died, I said to him, "Fred, why don't you speak to the captain when he comes to see you? He sure needs comfort and hope, for he blames himself for your injuries more than you think."

"I know it, Jim," said he, in a faint, low voice, "but I don't know how to begin, and before I can find the right words he's away."

Just as he said this the captain came below, and, going to the cot where Fred lay, took his hand in his, and tenderly spoke these words: "How do you feel now, my dear boy? Are you suffering much pain?"

"Not so much," replied Fred, then he looked anxiously into the captain's face.

"What would you like to say, my lad? You seem like you want to speak to me."

Fred smiled and said with laboring breath, "I'll soon be away, Captain—" He could not go on, but he pointed upward with his finger.

"Ah! You would tell me that the Lord of Heaven alone could give me comfort on earth. Is that your message to me?"

"Yes, Christ alone," cried Fred with a sudden and violent burst of energy. Moments later, he raised himself a little and seized the captain by the wrist. A short time passed before he was able to continue, but he turned to me, and said in a low voice: "Find the sixteenth chapter of Acts, verse thirty-one; also find Exodus, chapter twenty, verse eight. Read both to the captain—read both."

I quickly turned to the passages he mentioned, and read as follows, while Fred gazed earnestly into the captain's face.

"And they said, 'Believe on the Lord Jesus Christ and thou shalt be saved, and thy house. Remember the Sabbath day to keep it holy'."

"Will you believe in the Christ of Scripture, and will you remember to walk in His ways?" said the dying man, more earnestly.

"I will, I will indeed," replied Argus Flynn, while giant tears began to roll over his rugged cheeks. The captain felt a final firm grasp of his wrist by the dying sailor, who was trying to communicate his approval and joy.

Fred smiled faintly, but he did not speak again. He seemed to have received just enough strength to help lead a human soul to the Savior, and then he died. It was exactly one week after he had received his mortal wound.

We buried our shipmate in the usual sailor fashion. We wrapped him in his hammock, with a cannon ball at his feet to sink him. The captain read the burial service at the gangway, and then in deep silence, we committed his body to the deep.

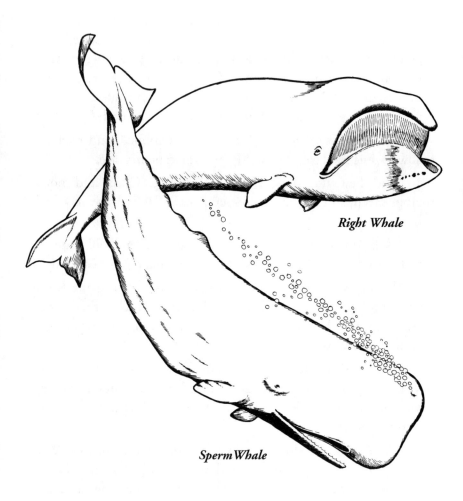

Right Whale

Sperm Whale

CHAPTER 11

A New Creature in Christ

The death of young Fred Hammer cast a gloom over the ship for many days. Everyone had respected, and many of us had loved, this simple man of God. But a sailor's life at sea is one of constant challenge and duty; therefore, he cannot afford to allow the sorrows of his heart to sit long upon his mind. For this reason, after several days of mourning, each man on board began to move past his grief and carry on with his work.

Whales soon began to appear around us as we started our journey back to New Bedford. The now familiar cry of "There she blows!" rang out frequently as the weeks past. Each time, we would hear the steady voice of the captain cry, "Where away?" and then, "Lower away." Then came the chase with all its dangers and excitement, followed by the striking of the mighty whale until, at last, it floated calmly on the sea.

During this time period, we all threw ourselves into our work in an effort to try to forget the sadness of recent days. But the hearts of one and all were not as light as before. Although none of us tried to show it, I knew full well that many a laugh was checked and many a joke was repressed, for the memory of our dead shipmate.

But the man who was most affected by Fred's death was the captain. This was natural and did not surprise us, but we were not prepared for the great change that soon appeared in his manner and conduct. After a time, he laughed with the rest of us at a good joke and cheered loudly when a big whale turned belly up. But his behavior toward us was more considerate and fatherly, and he entirely abandoned the habit of swearing. He also began to try to honor the Lord by respecting the Christian Sabbath. Many a whale did I see sporting and spouting near us on that day, but never again after our shipmate's death did we lower a boat or touch a harpoon on Sunday.

A few of the unsaved sailors on board used to swear against his policy and complain of it to each other. These men never spoke so as to let the captain hear, however, and they soon gave up their grumbling, for all of our crew had agreed to it when the captain first proposed the idea.

The first Sunday after Fred's death, the captain assembled our crew on the quarter-deck and spoke to us about his desire to limit our work on the Sabbath.

"Men," said Captain Flynn, "I've called you aft to make a proposal that may perhaps surprise you. Up to this point in our voyage, you know very well, there has been little difference aboard this ship between Saturday and Sunday. Since our shipmate Fred died, I have been thinkin' much on this matter. I've come to the conclusion that we should rest from all work on the Lord's Day, except those works that are necessary to keep the ship safe and sound. Now, men, I will not try to pretend that I am a wise theologian who has worked out exactly how the Sabbath should be kept and to what degree the Christian Sabbath is binding upon men today. This I do know, shipmates, that in times past I have neglected and despised my Maker, and in time to come I mean to try to respect Him and obey His commandments.

"When poor Fred was dying," continued the captain, "he asked me to promise that I would believe on the Lord Jesus Christ, and remember the Sabbath day, to keep it holy. I did promise, and, with the blessing of Almighty God, I mean to be a man of my word. Now, what think ye, men? Shall we give the whales a rest on Sunday?"

We all agreed to this proposal at once, for the effect of the captain's speech was great upon the entire crew. It was not so much what he said, as the earnest and heartfelt way in which he said it. When our bold and manly captain, who never flinched from danger or duty, began to speak tenderly of his love for Jesus Christ, it was difficult for many of us to believe our ears.

This was the final word from the captain about this matter; but in the days that followed, various members of the crew had many a hot discussion in the forecastle about this issue. Some men were in favor of the new move, and quickly defended the captain; while others called the captain an old woman and warned that our ship would never reach its quota.

In the course of time, however, we began to notice some very real benefits associated with the captain's new policy. Strengthened in body and spirit by resting one day, we possessed a greater vigor as we pursued our work the other six days. In our renewed strength we soon killed a number of whales under difficult circumstances, without losing one to the bottom of the ocean. The blessing of the Almighty could also be noted in that the general health of the crew improved and we had far fewer injuries or accidents. I firmly believe that all of these blessings were the direct result of God's promise to bless those who "call the Sabbath a delight; the holy of the Lord, honorable." (Isaiah 58:13)

One of the most memorable events in the entire voyage was the day that the captain celebrated God's goodness in helping us to fill our ship's hold with oil much sooner than expected. During this special celebration, the men who had been grumbling came forward and freely admitted that their concerns were baseless. The crowning event of the day, however, was when the ship's carpenter completed carving a special saying into the wooden plank over the captain's quarters, saying:

"Them that honor Me, I will honor."

As a result of all these events, every crew member that had the slightest spiritual promptings was now accustomed to looking for a blessing on the Sabbath. Obviously, however, the captain tried to remind the crew members that the true purpose for obeying any of God's commandments is not to obtain some specific temporal blessing, but to lay up spiritual treasures in heaven.

A new type of excitement began to blossom on board the *Landsman,* as the weeks flew by quickly and the men started to think of being reunited with family and friends. As our voyage was rapidly drawing to a close, the overall mood and tempo of the ship gradually changed. The sometimes tense and strict relationship that existed between the officers and common seamen became more relaxed. As each day went by, my songs became more focused upon the theme of returning home, in an attempt to keep the spirits of the men high.

More and more, the talk aboard the *Landsman* turned to the subject of what changes may have taken place in the world since

we all left civilization. One day, as a group of officers were playing checkers on the main deck, the lookout shouted: "Sail ho! Tall ship off the port bow. Looks to be a whaler of some kind, about two miles out."

As Captain Flynn came up on deck, one of the officers asked, "Sir, it looks like the bark *Superior*, likely under the command of Captain James Royce that is heading our way. Can we signal for a gam, sir?"

The captain thought on the idea for several moments, while he regularly sipped his coffee, sweetened with molasses. Finally, he responded, "Order the gam signal to be raised to the view of Captain Royce, and we shall see if he responds in kind."

A minute or two later, a signal flag was raised on the rigging of the *Superior* affirming their interest in participating in a gam.

"Square the yards. Look alive, my hearties!" yelled Captain Flynn, as he sought to slow the *Landsman*'s movement through the sea. Within a short period of time, our bark was settling down nicely in the water in preparation for dropping anchor.

CHAPTER 12

A Gam Brings News from Home

The sound of bells soon filled the air, as Captain Flynn called all hands to the main deck. He thanked the crew members for their hard work, and mentioned that he had decided to celebrate their accomplishments by giving them a chance to get together with some of the crew of the *Superior*.

"Hurrah, hurrah!" shouted the rowdy shipmates, as they received the captain's words. Twenty-two months at sea had created a hunger in the crew for fresh news from other seamen.

"Where does the *Superior* hale from, Captain?" questioned the second mate.

"She is out of Sag Harbor, and her captain trained with me years ago in Nantucket," answered Argus Flynn. Moments later he added, "The last time I shipped out with James Royce was when we sailed on his bark up the Bering Sea, and hunted bowhead whales in the chilly Arctic waters. Worst backgammon player I ever knew."

Mr. Owens, who was standing nearby, stated, "If it's outward bound that she be then, Captain, chances are that these sailors will be able to give us fresh news from home. They probably just left New England about a fortnight ago."

"Well, it may be your hopes of fresh news will be realized, Mr. Owens," responded the captain. "But I should think that they have been outward bound for longer than a fortnight."

The sound of seagulls interrupted the closing words of Argus Flynn, as the crew eagerly awaited word about who would join the captain in his long boat journey over to the *Superior*, which was anchored nearby.

"Mr. Owens," called the captain, "let the men draw sticks to see who is to join me on my trip over to Captain Royce. The six men who draw the shortest sticks will accompany me."

"Aye, aye, sir," responded the first mate.

Several minutes later, a half-dozen men with smiling faces, including myself, came strutting up to the gangway and prepared for the order to get into the captain's boat.

"Take to your oars, men, and prepare to lower away," called the captain as he turned to his first mate. "You are in charge in my absence, Mr. Owens, so look well to your duty. Set the watch with diligence, and signal me at the first sign of trouble or foul weather.

"I will take good care of the *Landsman* and her crew until you return, Captain," the first mate assured him.

Before long, the captain and his picked crew were pulling their way across the water toward the neighboring ship. It only took about five minutes for us to row the short distance over to the *Superior*.

As we approached Captain Royce's bark, Argus Flynn softly said, "Ship your oars, men, and prepare to secure the bow line."

One of the sailors from the *Superior* suddenly leaned over the side and yelled, "Can I throw ye a line, sir?"

"Aye, mate," called Captain Flynn. "Ye better fit us out with two lines, fore and aft, for the wind is contrary and the sea choppy."

"Very well, Captain Flynn," confirmed the young sailor.

After the boat was secured, Captain Flynn climbed up the side of the ship that led to the main deck and called out, loud and clear, "Requesting permission from the officer in charge to come aboard."

"Permission granted," uttered James Royce, as he finished walking over to the place where Captain Flynn was climbing over the railing of the ship.

"Why, you old sea dog, how are you this fine day?" questioned the newly arrived guest.

"Never better, my old shipmate," came the quick response. "But it is my need to ask ye, what are ye here for, Captain?"

Without hesitation, Captain Flynn recited the traditional response of whale men. "I'm here for whales, oil, and hard work."

"Very well then, Captain. Ye be welcome aboard this whaler," said James Royce with a broad grin.

After a lively handshake between the two captains, James Royce gave the order for his first mate to take a group of sailors from the *Superior* to the *Landsman*. A short time later, Captain Royce yelled over in the direction of the galley. "Look lively now, cook. Our guests need their ration of plum duff and coffee."

As the captains continued to enjoy the process of getting reacquainted, the common sailors exchanged stories, as well as books and newspapers. It did not take long before I turned the discussion to the topic of recent events in New England. "What news have ye about old New Bedford town?" I asked.

One of the sailors from the *Superior* quickly stated, "Ye ought to know that New Bedford town seldom changes these days. The talk of New England at this time is the ending of the Mexican War by a treaty signed early this year. It looks like our country may gain control over the territories of California and New Mexico."

"What do you mean, we won the war in Mexico?" I asked. "I did not even know that our country was in a war south of the border. We shipped out in the early part of 1846."

My shipmate, Ben Lodins, continued the discussion by asking, "What other details can ye tell us of the war?"

"Well," uttered the other sailor, "our fighting men under General Scott managed to storm Mexico City in the fall, and the Mexican government sued for peace. Not all of the citizens of New England, however, were happy about our victory. The famous author, Henry David Thoreau, from Massachusetts, is speaking out against the war. He claims that the conflict is more about extending slavery than anything else. In fact, Mr. Thoreau recently spent a night in jail due to his refusal to pay a poll tax to help pay for the recent war in Mexico."

"And how about some of the new inventions?" I questioned. "Has Samuel Morse done anything more with that talking wire telegraph he demonstrated a few years back?"

"Precious little," responded one of the officers from Captain Royce's ship. "It's not clear whether Morse's magic wire will get much use in New England, but, according to the newspapers, he remains hopeful."

As the sun rose higher in the sky, the atmosphere aboard the *Superior* became increasingly jovial. While new friendships were being made, the cook finally appeared on deck with mugs of plum pudding and a batch of rice cakes. It did not take long for us to finish up these special treats.

While our second mate was in the middle of a humorous yarn, Captain Royce ordered all hands to come to the foredeck. As we stood around waiting for the captain's words, we soon heard him shout, "I want every soul on board to know that I am officially challenging Captain Flynn to a game of backgammon!"

"Oh, for the love of whales," groaned Argus Flynn.

"The loser of this contest between captains," continued James Royce, "will be obliged to shine the shoes of every sailor on board the *Superior*."

"Hurrah, hurrah!" bellowed the men, with gusto.

"Very well, very well," agreed Captain Flynn, who then added, "you have not beaten me in any previous contest, but I suppose there is a first time for everything."

A hush fell over the deck, as the two men began their all important contest. For the next two hours, all you could hear was the munching of rice cakes and the snickering of various members of the assembly. Finally, after the sun had begun to set, a simple question could be heard rising from the deck of the *Superior*. Captain Flynn asked his opponent, "So, when can I expect to see you take up your old hobby of shining boots, Captain?"

"All in good time, my ungracious guest," came the reply. "You would think after all these years that I would take up another game, but I must first find a way to beat you, at least once."

"Well, I admire your determination," said Captain Flynn, "but I think you would be better off using your determination for whaling, instead of backgammon."

The next instant, several of the men began to join me in singing a well known chantey, much to the satisfaction of Captain Royce. As the evening wore on, the air became filled with a steady stream of rowdy songs and hilarious stories. Only fatigue prevented our gam from continuing on past the midnight hour.

As the men prepared to settle into their bunks, Captain Royce gave his orders to those on watch and headed for his quarters. Captain Flynn crawled into the bunk normally occupied by the first mate, and was soon fast asleep.

The next morning dawned brightly, as the second watch of the day took their positions on board. The breeze had slackened over the hours of the night, and we were all enjoying fair weather and warm hospitality.

As Captain Flynn walked the deck, he soon came across the path of his former backgammon rival. After a brief smile, he began, "Good morning, your excellency, how has your shoe shining been progressing?"

"Well enough, my curious friend," came the reply. "So when are you going to tell me about how your whaling game has gone these past two years?" added Captain Royce.

"The Almighty has been gracious to us, very gracious," began the captain in a sincere tone. "We have filled our hold to capacity slightly ahead of schedule, and we have only had one fatality."

"I see," responded Captain Royce. "When are you hoping to reach New Bedford?"

"My plan is to make sail this afternoon, with the hope of reaching port in about two weeks. Do you think we can reach home in this time, if the winds are favorable?"

"Quite likely, Captain," responded James Royce, "but we will miss out on the opportunity to finish our next round of backgammon."

"Lord willing, we can take care of that detail when we meet again. In the meantime, you have big whales to catch and blubber to process," concluded Captain Flynn.

"True enough, my old friend," said the captain of the *Superior*.

An hour or two later, Captain Flynn could be heard saying, "Prepare our boat for launch, men. Stow your gear and be ready on my order."

We all nodded in recognition of the captain, but in truth, none of us wanted the gam to end so soon. The two captains bid each other farewell and Godspeed amidst a carefully concealed veil of tears. Before we left the *Superior*, however, Captain Flynn presented a special gift to James Royce in recognition of his hospitality. As Captain Royce began to open his gift, a rising tide of laughter soon broke forth on board, for the present was a new kit for shining shoes.

As the wind began to stiffen, we quickly completed our final preparations for getting underway. Upon the order of Captain Flynn, we soon found ourselves dipping our oars in the water in an effort to get back to our ship. On our way back, we met the men from the *Superior* who had just completed their gam on the *Landsman*. As our boats passed each other amidships, each crew let out a parting cheer and continued on its way with a light heart.

CHAPTER 13
Home at Last

As we prepared to take the *Landsman* on the final leg of her homeward bound journey, the first mate was busy organizing groups of men who would be responsible for cleaning certain areas of the ship. After almost two years at sea, the *Landsman* was in need of some sprucing up.

During the latter part of the day, after we had gotten underway, the captain made a point of visiting with each work party to inspect its progress. "Make her shine, lads. The owners expect me to return their boat in good order," remarked the seasoned skipper. "Mr. Owens," he continued, "I am going to my cabin to work on my log and journal. Trim the sails and set our course for home."

"Aye, sir," answered the first mate.

As I finished waxing the area near the helm, I asked Mr. Owens why a captain needed to keep a logbook. He thought for a few moments and then responded, "Shipmate, a captain must give an account of his gains to those he is working for. A captain must keep an accurate tally of the number of barrels of oil on board, the type of whales that were captured and the location in which each whale was taken. These records not only enable the owners to clearly see how their ship performed at sea, but can also provide invaluable information by which future voyages can be governed. Whales, as ye know, tend to be creatures of habit and often swim in the same waters year after year."

Before long, it was evening on board the *Landsman,* as many of the sailors busied themselves by making final preparations for arriving in New Bedford. Most of the men took to having their hair cut, and some even went so far as to bathe with soap. As the evening meal was being passed out, I determined to get caught up with the mending of my jacket and pants. After my efforts were completed, however, it reminded me of just how much I missed my dear mother.

Unlike the early months at sea, I seldom thought of my mother unless some circumstance would spark my memory. Now that we were just days away from port, however, my mind began, once again, to think about her. Was she prospering? Did she survive the lonely nights with a stout heart? As I thought on these things, I comforted my heart with the knowledge that I would soon know the answer to these questions.

Before going on watch, Ben Lodins came up to me and asked, "So how are ye going to spend your share of money, Jim?"

Never having given it much thought, I said, "The first part of my money will go to paying for those who took care of my widowed mother these two years. Whatever is left over, I hope to use in the purchase of a piece of land for myself."

"Just be careful of land sharks," warned my shipmate, wryly.

"What are land sharks, if ye don't mind me askin'?" said I, with a strange expression on my face.

"Why, they are clever salesmen sent out by the merchants and outfitters in town. Their sole duty is to persuade you to purchase something substantial on the spur of the moment, before you can get your wits about you. They may also try to get you to sign on for another whaling voyage."

"Oh, I see," was my response. "Thanks for the tip, mate. I will beware of those vermin."

After I completed my so-called "dogwatch", which lasted well past midnight, I retired to my bunk and quickly fell asleep. Six hours later, I awoke from a restless sleep to the sound of a hymn. Much to my surprise, the captain had decided to join with a few of the men in a rousing chorus of "Blest Be the Tie That Binds." As I finished dressing, the sweet sounds of a familiar song of praise were soon replaced by the gravely voice of the second mate, who shouted, "All hands on deck!"

I quickly made my way topside and joined the men who were gathered together toward the stern of the ship. Moments later, Captain Flynn proceeded to fulfill his pledge by awarding the sailor who was responsible for spotting Big Tom with the two gold coins. As this middle-aged sailor examined his treasure, he smiled so hard that I thought that his face would break. Before dismissing the assembly, Argus Flynn added, "Men, our journey is almost over. We have all learned many things as we have sailed together and fought with whales. Let us finish our voyage with integrity and ask the Almighty to guide us safely home to our loved ones. For your safety, I have ordered Mr. Owens to double the watch so as to keep a sharp eye out for rocks. I expect you all to cooperate with this order. Return to your posts, men."

The next three days at sea were cloudy and windy. It was only with great difficulty that the helmsman was able to keep the *Landsman* fairly on course.

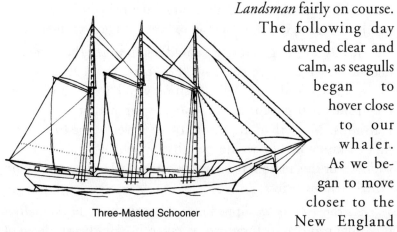

Three-Masted Schooner

The following day dawned clear and calm, as seagulls began to hover close to our whaler. As we began to move closer to the New England coast, our lookouts began to spot an increasing number of small fishing vessels in addition to outbound whalers of every sort. All of these sights and sounds served to boost the expectation that each man on board had that New Bedford was near. No longer did the officers need to require men to stand watch, for nearly every seaman on board was stationed somewhere along the perimeter of the *Landsman,* eagerly scanning the horizon.

Finally, after what seemed like an eternity, the lookout bellowed, "Land ho!"

The first landmass that we spotted was the familiar island of Nantucket. A short time later, we passed Martha's Vineyard. Captain Flynn then or-

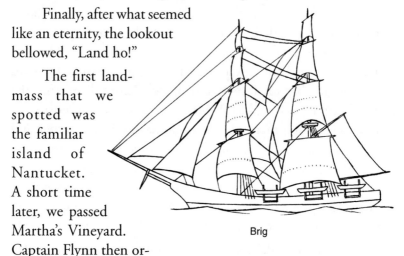

Brig

dered our final turn toward the harbor of New Bedford. As the grand old lighthouse, which stood prominently in the harbor, came clearly into view, our hearts began to beat with greater intensity.

It was not long before we could begin to see the two-story mansions, which towered above the wharf. For several generations, the wives of New Bedford stood watch for incoming vessels from small platforms, which were perched atop these tall mansions. More than anything, those wives wished to be the first to know if they would be a happy whale man's wife or a widow. For this reason, the small rooftop decks were commonly called "widow walks."

As the *Landsman* slipped into the main body of the harbor, the captain ordered all sails to be taken in. He then ordered all hands to prepare the ship for docking. As the *Landsman* began to be prepared for a well-deserved rest, crowds could be seen rushing to the waterfront. News had spread through town that Captain Flynn's bark had appeared in the harbor, and, as usual, such a report generated excitement.

After our beloved ship was tied fast to the dock, Captain Flynn took several minutes to say farewell to the men under his command. I well remember the words that were exchanged between us that day, as he came before me. We began with a hearty hug, and then I asked, "Well, Captain, it has been a voyage I will never forget. It does not seem possible that our task is at an end. What will you do now, sir?"

"As captain of this ship, I still have one unfinished piece of business to take care of," asserted Argus Flynn soberly. "It is my duty to make contact with Fred Hammer's mother so as to inform her of the fate of her son."

"Would you like me to join you, Captain?" I asked.

"No, mate," he said. "This is one job that belongs to me alone. Pray that I will have the courage to tell her the whole truth."

"Very well, Captain," I said. "Until we meet again, may the Lord bless you and keep you in the palm of His hand."

Several minutes passed before I could gather up the remainder of my gear and make my way to shore. When I finally reached the wharf, I was not surprised by the fact that my mother was absent from those standing amidst the crowd. As I continued to walk up Water Street with my shipmate, Tim Dronner, he suddenly stopped and turned in my direction.

"What's the matter?" I asked.

"I almost forgot," he began. "A messenger stopped me a few minutes ago when we came ashore and gave me this note. It is addressed to you, Jim."

"So it is," I responded. "I wonder what it is about."

"In these situations, mate, you generally don't know until you open the letter and read it!"

"I suppose you are right, Tim. You always were the one with the sharp mind," came the reply.

"Before you get any older, then, please open the note!" said Tim, with an impatient tone.

Tim stared at me as I quickly read the note, and then he asked, "Well, now what does it say?"

"It directs me to go promptly to the Seaman's Bethel upon my arrival. Strange, though, for it gives no further explanation."

"I hope everything is alright with your mother, shipmate," said Tim tenderly. "Do you want me to go with you?"

"No thanks, friend," said I, "for whatever the situation may be I am sure that Reverend Carlson can help me sort it out."

Amidst tears and hugs, Tim and I went our separate ways. It was difficult to part with a shipmate after so long of a journey together. Nevertheless, the afternoon was coming on and I needed to try to locate my mother and discover her condition.

It seemed strange to be trodding the streets of New Bedford once again. Thankfully, however, it did not take long for me to get my bearings and locate the correct path to the Seaman's Bethel. On my way up to Johnnycake Hill, I stopped at a store on Union Street to pick up an apple and a bag of nuts to munch on. I had not eaten in hours and it had been months since I had tasted fresh fruit of any kind. These simple items seemed like great luxuries to me, as did the taste of fresh water, for such things were often hard to come by at sea.

After my pint-sized meal was finished, I proceeded to the parsonage of Rev. Carlson. Numerous thoughts began to flood upon my mind as I approached the residence of my friend and pastor. Was my mother safe in Fairhaven or was she ill and boarding in New Bedford? Was my mother even alive at all? I wondered. If she was safe and well how would I get a ride over to see her? As I continued to ponder these questions, I walked up to the parsonage and knocked on the front door.

A few moments passed before the door began to swing open. I was both shocked and pleased to find that the woman who stood before me was none other than my mother. Shouts of joy soon could be heard in every direction as my mother embraced me as only a mother can. She then spoke to me, saying, "My, how you have grown into manhood, my dear son, since you sailed away. You are, indeed, a sight for sore eyes."

"I, I, did not expect to see you here and now, Mother," I said in a stammering fashion. "But it is grand to be able to see you straight off, without having to hitch a ride out to your home in Fairhaven."

"Well, you might as well know, now, that I no longer live in Fairhaven," stated my mother directly.

"Oh, Mother, are things unwell?" I questioned. "Did you lose the old homestead?"

"Rest easy, my son, although our old home is gone things are very well, indeed."

As my mother was finishing her mystifying statement, Rev. Carlson made his appearance at the door. "Woman," he said, "don't you think it would be proper to invite your long lost son into his new home before he gets any more confused by your remarks?"

"New home, no longer live in Fairhaven?" I muttered. "Would someone kindly tell me what is going on?"

"All in good time, James, please come in and sit yourself down," urged the kindly parson. "It is a little difficult to know where to begin telling you of how things are at present. So much has changed, James, since you sailed away on Captain Flynn's bark."

"Well, for starters," I said, "what kind of care did you give my poor widowed mother in my absence that would cause her to lose her home. When I was here last, at least she had a roof over her head."

"Your mother has received the best care of any woman in New England, of that you can be certain. In regard to her having a roof over her head, I guess it might be most fitting to say that she simply exchanged her old roof for a new one. You see, James," said the preacher, "your mother and I are now married and living under the same roof."

"You mean to tell me, that my mother is your wife?" I said while scratching my head.

"Yes, James," he responded with a grin. "And it would also stand to reason that I would be your new father, if you will have me. Spending time with your mother caused me, in the providence of God, to grow in my admiration and affection for her many excellent qualities."

After a few seconds of thought, I stated, "If I can trust you as a temporary caregiver, there seems to be no reason for me not to trust you as a permanent one. By the look of contentment on my mother's face, it surely seems that you must have been giving her lots of loving care."

"Indeed he has," inserted my mother, "there were times after your father passed away, James, when I thought that I may never find a suitable man to fill his shoes. Thank God that my thinking was wrong. I have learned, once again, never to underestimate the power of the Almighty."

"So, how long has it been since you tied the bands?" I asked.

"Very nearly ten months, James," answered my newly discovered stepfather. "It is like I have always told you, God works in mysterious ways, His wonders to perform."

"Obviously, I regret not being here for the wedding ceremony," I added. "Yet it is a comfort knowing that my mother will be well cared for should I ever decide to seek my fortune at sea in the days ahead."

"At least, I hope that you will stick around our home long enough to let us fatten you up a bit before you venture out on another ship," pleaded my mother.

"I will try my level best to ignore the call of the sea for as long as possible, dear madam, but now that my passion has been stirred for high sea adventure it can only be but a brief season before I again go fighting with whales."

CHAPTER 14

Old Glory and New Dreams

"So that is how my first voyage to the South Seas ended. As you might expect, in later years, Tim and I made many more trips as whaling men, both in the north and south. But I have already tried your patience, dear townfolk, in being so long-winded about my first adventure as a whale man. I will, therefore, spare you from having to listen to any more stories about the bygone days of whaling.

"This more I will only say, that my life as a whale man brought me into many dangers, but the Lord has preserved me safe through them all. Yea, and further still, He has preserved my soul in the midst of trials of a far worse kind than one's body falls in with while fighting whales."

The little group that had been listening to me so attentively for several hours seemed to suddenly come alive with questions. One young man finally summoned the courage to ask, "Why has whaling gone away from New Bedford? Are most of the whales gone from the seas?"

I pondered these questions for several moments, and then answered: "New Bedford's greatest year for whaling was 1857. At this time, during the glory days, ten thousand men were making their living in the whaling industry. As amazing as it may seem right now, Bedford town once had over three hundred and twenty whalers registered in its fleet, bringing in vast quantities of oil and bone.

"As to what caused the whaling business to fade away from

New Bedford and the surrounding ports of New England, you must realize that many factors were involved. First of all, and perhaps most importantly, "rock oil" or petroleum was discovered in 1859 in Pennsylvania. This new discovery dramatically affected the demand for whale oil, as more and more people began to use petroleum and natural gas in place of the expensive oil that came from whales. The second reason centered upon the destruction of large numbers of whaling ships during the War Between the States and in the Arctic Fleet disasters of the 1870s. In just these two instances, well over one hundred whalers were destroyed, causing tremendous financial loss for ship owners.

"To add to the growing problems associated with the business of whaling, it was simply getting more difficult to find whales. Not that whales were totally swept from the seas during the late nineteenth century, but a number of the species of whales were, not withstanding, severely over hunted. In light of all this, the typical cost of underwriting a whaling voyage become more expensive for the ships had to travel farther, with bigger crews, only to capture a decreasing number of giant mammals.

"The ultimate reason for the shrinking of the whaling industry, however, was the simple fact that people no longer needed whale oil and bone. No profit can come to ship owners if they invest in the procuring of whale products if there is but little demand."

As I finished answering the first lad's questions, another young man in the crowd asked, "Did you ever feel bad about killing whales just to get oil that could have come from someplace else?"

"In the early days of whaling, before the invention of ocean going steamships and powerful cannon-powered whaling guns, I never felt ashamed of my work as a whaler. We were providing a valuable and necessary product for the good of man, without endangering the whale population in any significant way.

"As time passed by, however, I saw first-hand how the glory days of whaling in the era of sailing vessels turned into the impersonal slaughtering of animals that were no longer needed for oil or for much else. The wholesale killing of whales in the sanctuary of the Arctic is a classic example of what has gone wrong with whaling in the recent past. As a matter of simple stewardship and common decency, it does not make sense for whales to be hunted to extinction.

"As much as we all should deplore the foolish excesses of the whaling industry in the late nineteenth century, these concerns should not be allowed to tarnish the brave and legitimate accomplishments of those men who sailed in earlier days after monsters of the deep armed only with a simple spear and Yankee courage."

At this point, the crowd that had set itself around my table was fast beginning to disperse. Much to my delight, a number of those in the inn made a point of telling me how grateful they were for the chance to learn the true story of whaling. A feeling of relief soon flooded my soul, as I realized that I had finally told a story that the younger generation needed to hear.

My old friend, Tim Dronner, tipped his hat to the last of the townspeople to go on their way, after which he sat down and said, "Well, my good man, you have gotten something very important off of your chest. Now that the deed is done, what say ye to partaking of one of those bowls of chowder that the proprietor keeps harping about? I've developed a powerful hunger while listening to your chatter."

"Tim, my old friend," I remarked, "now that I have told the story of our lives as whale men, I may go at any time to meet my Maker in perfect peace. By all means, bring on the chowder, for it is no longer to be feared."

The End

—*Bibliography*—

Ashley, Clifford W. *The Yankee Whaler*
New York, Dover Publications, 1938.

Ballantyne, R. M. *Fighting the Whales*
New York, 1880.

Block, Irvin. *The Real Book About Ships*
New York, Garden City Books, 1953.

Melville, Herman. *Moby Dick.*

Pease, Zephaniah W. *The History of New Bedford*
New York, The Lewis Historical Publishing
Company, 1918.

Reinfeld, Fred. *Whales and Whaling*
New York, Garden City Books, 1960.

Sanderson, Ivan T. *Follow the Whale*
Boston, Little Brown, 1956.

Shapiro, Irwin. *The Story of Yankee Whaling*
New York, American Heritage Publishers, 1959.

Whipple, A.B.C. *Yankee Whalers in the South Seas*
New York, Doubleday, 1954.